Karily

An Allert Village Novel
By
Kristy Woods

Published by Kristy Woods
Copyright © Kristy Woods, 2015

Cover Design by Charlotte Lipp
Copyright © Charlotte Lipp, 2015

www.kristywoods.com

This book is dedicated to my mother, Patricia Maureen Bennett, who recognized at a very early age that the "social awkwardness" I exhibited was not a phase.

So she took me by the hand, led me up the stairs to the West branch Lincoln Library in Springfield, Illinois and introduced me to the magical world of books. She accepted the fact that I was much more comfortable in a room surrounded by books than by people.

In my teens, she presented me with her Brother manual typewriter and said simply "Write."

So I did.

Thanks mom.

Love,
Your late bloomer

Prologue

Just over the crest of Allert Hill, in the village lake, through the early morning mist, ducks float, then dip, then rise to wander choreographed confusion before lighting once again simply to float, dip and rise.

Each morning as she watched the daily dance, Karilyne wondered if the ducks were happy or if they were as restless in their seemingly endless search as she was.

To all who knew her, she appeared the epitome of serenity, floating calmly only to dip occasionally when absolutely necessary, but always returning to the surface strong and assured. What none of them ever witnessed were the times when she rose high, higher, seeking direction just as the ducks did, searching for a sign, for something just beyond the mist.

She sat riveted to the wrought iron hummingbird

bench, the only seat you would find if you happened to stumble upon the quiet little pond on the outskirts of Allert Village. If you got there early enough, you might also see Karilyne, her arms outstretched directly in front of her, palms up, fingers cupped as though waiting for an answer to fall into her hands. She had been convinced on one of these mornings that she felt her mother's presence and since then had begun to talk to the fog that blanketed her and the bench.

The days have finally begun to cool. Fall is my favorite time of the year. Remember when I was a kid and I spent all of those hours lying in the back yard covered with iodined baby oil and lemon juiced hair in my candy striped bikini praying for boobs? Wanting so desperately to be grown up! I thought grown- ups had all of the answers.

Karilyne leaned back against the bench and squinted through quilted maple leaves at a brilliant fall sun.

I am beginning to worry that this is going to be the rest of my life. I am frightened by the prospect of never really being happy again and I am just not sure I can take that. I thought by now there would some understanding... some peace... some knowing. I thought I would know who I was and what it all meant, but I am more uncertain now than I have ever been. So much of my life has been because of something you taught me. Things you said and did most often when you weren't even aware that I was watching or listening and now I have no idea if any of it was right. Did anything I do matter? I tried to be a good mother and a good wife, but I can only think of the mistakes I made.

The ducks had begun their lazy waddle up the bank and towards the bench hearing Karilyne's voice and assuming bits of stale bread would accompany it. Karilyne smiled, *Sorry guys, I have nothing for you... or me.*

Fall

Chapter One

Karilyne stood in front of the red brick building with the For Sale sign in the window. She pulled her jacket tightly around her small frame as a gust of wind whipped around the corner and autumns first leaves, umber and golden, floated softly to the ground around her.

The original small paned windows, like something out of a Dickens novel, remained intact. Karilyne had done a little research at the village library and had discovered that the building had been built in the late 1800's and, for the most part, had not been tampered with. Other than electrical, heating and cooling updates, the integrity of the original structure remained, including the hardwood plank floors. It had been a grocery store so the design was simple. Two rooms, one in the front to display wares and a back room for storage and larger items.

A small bathroom had been added when indoor plumbing had arrived in the village.

Karilyne fished through her jeans pocket and found the key that Mr. Norman had given her two weeks earlier when she had casually asked about the building. "Take your time, " he had said. "Go through it, have it inspected, whatever you need and then get back to me." It had taken her two weeks to work up the nerve to actually decide to set a foot inside.

She jiggled the door handle and, after a couple of tugs, the door swung open. She stood for just a moment, allowing the crisp fall air to circulate through the front room before closing the door behind her. Surprisingly, the floors appeared to need only a good sweeping and polishing. The ceilings were high and begging for fans. The interior walls were the same red brick as the exterior walls and seemed to be in fairly good condition.

Karilyne wandered into the back room and found it
to be equal to the front room in size and condition.
Light was limited as the only windows were those
across the front of the building. Karilyne turned the
deadbolt on the back door. Sun light and the wild
ivy that grew haphazardly across the back of the
building poured in. She smiled "perfect." A small
yard surrounded by a picket fence in need of repair
or removal stretched from the back of the building
to the alley.

Karilyne smiled and thought of the summers she
had spent with her grandmother when she was a
little girl. Her love of cooking and gardening had
come for the most part from her Grandma Grace.
Their days were adventurous and special and, at
night in the attic room filled with the memories of
her mother's childhood, Grandma Grace would
tuck her in with the quilt that Karilyne's great-
grandmother had made and say "We sure made a
memory today!"

Many afternoons were spent simply sitting inside the branches of a huge weeping willow tree on a blanket that bore their ancestors' tartan colors eating freshly baked scones while Grace taught her Scottish songs and Gaelic phrases.

One particular Saturday afternoon, Grace presented Karilyne with a bonnet, donned one herself, and the two of them took a rare trip into the city to visit a tea room, and that was it… it was all Karilyne wanted. She wanted a tea room of her own. Through high school, college, marriage and children, she dreamed about the little tea room where tea was warm and comforting and the chocolate cake was soulful.

 'Am I crazy? Do I really want this or is this just a way to fill the emptiness now that the kids are gone and Jake is so busy with his work' She shut the door and walked back into the front room running her fingers along the uneven bricks. *'I flip through my date book and I see dates that I used to look forward to and now*

they are just one more day. I walk through an empty house and I wonder where the time went. Did I do a good job? I rarely hear from the kids. Jake says they're busy and I know he's right, after all, didn't I say that it was my job to raise healthy happy, independent people? I guess I just didn't realize how lonely it would be.'

She stood in the middle of the front room and closed her eyes and pictured tables covered with antique linens. She could almost smell the kitchen aromas from the fresh baked breads and pots of simmering soups. The small yard, overflowing with vegetables and herbs just waiting to be picked and used in her creations.

Karilyne locked the front door and slid the key into her pocket. She took one last look and made her decision, the decision she knew she was going to make long before she had walked through the front door.

She called Mr. Norman and made arrangements to meet him at the bank the following morning to finalize paperwork.

She told Jake about her new venture and he smiled. "All I want is for you to be happy Karilyne and if this makes you happy, then I am happy for you. Now, what can I do to help?"

It took three short weeks to open. Jake called the contractor that his architectural firm used so often and, because the building was so sound, minimal work had to be done to bring it to code. Karilyne had dug through the cedar chest her mother had given her and found the old folder with the café pictures she had clipped and saved when she had first begun to dream of having a place of her own. She installed ceiling fans and scoured antique shops for the front room tables, chairs, linens and knotty pine coat racks. She was warned that if she didn't replace the front windows, her heating bill might suffer, but she couldn't do it, she was willing to pay the extra to keep the quaint store front where she could display her cakes and pies.

She readied the kitchen, purchased ingredients and on October 10th, the day of her 45th birthday, Karilyne's Korner opened for business.

Karilyne took a deep breath, took one more look at the dining room, unlocked the door and turned the sign from CLOSED to OPEN.

The menu was simple, unique soups using the herbs she grew, spices she ordered and a variety of wines and Sherries. Small date nut sandwiches accompanied each steaming bowl.

She was a mediocre baker, although people clamored for her chocolate lavender tart, what it lacked in appearance, it all but made up for in deep, rich chocolate with a hint of lavender but she soon discovered that a tea room cannot live on soups and chocolate alone.

She placed an ad in the local paper and one chilly November day the bell above the door rang out and a slim, young woman carrying a set of whisks, brightly colored bowls, and a set of measuring spoons, walked into the dining room.

"I've come for the job. I assume the kitchen is in the back."

And with that she had walked straight past Karilyne into the tiny kitchen and begun to take inventory.

Karilyne was speechless and simply listened in between trips to the dining room as Jaclyn tskd her way through the cupboards.

By the end of her first day, she had a list of ingredients and a dessert menu that rivaled the Russian tea room's.

When Jaclyn was in the fourth grade, her mother took her by the hand and quietly explained to what the word divorce meant and how it was going to become a part of her life. Divorce meant no more shouting, no more arguing, and those were good things her mother had said, although Jaclyn had learned to tune out the ugly words and the soft sobbing that seeped into the walls and became a part of the very foundation upon which she lived. Divorce also meant moving to Chicago, where her mother would now work. But mostly, and all Jaclyn heard, was that divorce meant no more Sunday mornings alone with Dad in the vintage pickup truck that the two of them had restored, riding through Allert village, waving, calling good mornings and eating the chocolate frosted cake donuts that were forbidden beyond the picket fence that framed the yellow bungalow. Divorce meant she would no longer be able to look into the eyes that looked exactly like hers.

Divorce meant not knowing who she was anymore. In Chicago, Jaclyn became a latch key kid. Her mother worked long hours and attended night school two nights a week. She explained to Jaclyn that all of the hard work would pay off and ensure them of a better life, but Jaclyn knew only that it meant a lot of time alone. Her television access was very limited. Her mother locked out anything that wasn't educational. Jaclyn soon convinced her that cooking was part of a well-rounded education so her mother allowed the cooking channel. Weekly, Jaclyn gave her mother a list of necessary ingredients and what her mother deemed unnecessary or too expensive, Jaclyn simply "borrowed" from the other tenants with an understanding that her creations would be shared. She soon discovered that she was at her best with flour and sugar and after hours of practicing with a pastry bag and cheap frosting she became an expert at decorating. When extra money was needed for her and her mother, she sold small, personalized cakes to the tenants and their families. White almond frosting served as the background for roses and tulips, the flowers that had bloomed faithfully along the picket fence of what had been her home in Allert village. Daisies and daffodils, the flowers that had blanketed the fields that surrounded the village. With time and patience she had even begun to create tiny marzipan birds; yellow finches, bluebirds, cardinals, the birds that seemed never to visit the fourth floor of their apartment building. She dreamt of her creations on display in a famous bakery or featured in the windows of a Parisian patisserie but for now, it was a way to pass the long lonely hours she spent in the tiny apartment.

Junior High and High School dragged by. Jaclyn was not able to participate in extracurricular activities. No dances, no clubs, no dating...although that had not proved to be a big problem as she had never been asked. Immediately after school, she caught the bus home and remained there until it was time to catch the morning bus back to school. She graduated from high school and immediately got a job at a small bakery. She was in heaven! Surrounded by mixers, ovens and sacks of flour and sugar, Jaclyn was able to create desserts that brought long lines to the little bakery.

Her second love was vintage anything and when she had spare change, she often spent it on vintage hankies and aprons, creating stories about the person that might have owned them. People who lived in little yellow houses with white picket fences... not apartment buildings with dark hallways and bolted doors.

One afternoon, on one of her rare days off, she stumbled upon a set of brightly colored 1950's Pyrex mixing bowls and knew she had to have them. The set of five was $120.00 but after promising that she would personally deliver Holiday cakes to the owners' family, she bought the set for $50.00, all that she had on her. She walked the twelve blocks home with her treasure and they were one of the few things she had returned to Allert village with when her ailing father had asked that they get to know one another before it was too late. She agreed, knowing that it meant sacrificing her dream. She knew there would be no job for a baker in the small village and then one blustery afternoon, as Jaclyn sat alone on the Allert pond's bench reading the village newsletter, fate came to call:

WANTED: BAKER see Karilyne at Karilyne's Korner.

She gathered up her bowls and her moxie and the rest, well, was history.

"You can do all of this?" Karilyne asked as she read through the list.

"I wouldn't have put it on the list if I couldn't." Jaclyn said, perplexed. "I'll need money for the shopping."

Karilyne began to say that she could certainly handle the shopping but stopped short knowing that this culinary tornado would not be satisfied with any of the products Karilyne would buy so she simply gave her the money.

"Thanks, I'll be back tonight."

"We're not open at night," began Karilyne.

"*You* may not be but I'll need to get started on the doughs and cheesecakes. The apple cakes are always better the next day," she hollered over her shoulder as she walked back through the door she had entered only two hours earlier.

Karilyne sat down heavily into her mother's antique rocker. The dining room now empty she breathed in the aroma of that day's work, looked at the stack of dishes that needed to be done and realized she had not even gotten the name of her new pastry chef, "Oh my... what have I gotten myself into!"

Chapter Two

Karilyne met Jake Callahan at a poetry reading on a snowy January evening in a small coffee shop just off campus. They had actually been seated across the room from each other and met when they had both been asked to leave for laughing at the poet. They found themselves standing on the sidewalk underneath a blinking coffee cup, mimicking the poet and laughing like two idiots. They wandered the streets, catching snow on their tongues and relating the stories of their young lives and what they hoped for their future.

Jake was studying art and architecture and Karilyne's passions were music and literature. Anyone who saw them together, sighed with audible envy. Karilyne's auburn hair cascading down Jake's strong back as she sat with her head on his shoulder, his dark hair brushing her cheek. They were inseparable and, one year to the day they met, he proposed to her on one knee in the campus gazebo as the snow fell in tiny flakes on the tips of their red noses.

They laid out a well thought out plan; graduate, marry, build their dream home and careers, then, when Jake's architectural business was well established… children.

Things had not gone exactly as planned. While in the midst of building their dream home, they discovered Karilyne was pregnant so instead of pursuing her dream as a concert musician, she taught music at the local grade school and instead of opening his own architectural firm, Jake accepted a position with a well-established "safe" firm. It was, of course, to have been temporary.

Karilyne was so ecstatic with the birth of their children that she rarely spoke about the career she was so certain she would pursue after graduation. Motherhood and teaching were a perfect fit. The only person who seemed to be deeply disappointed was Karilyne's mother leaving Jake to wonder if it

had been Karilyne's dream… or her mother's.

They were happy… or so he thought, but things

were changing.

Jake Callahan was losing his wife… and he knew it.

He just didn't know what to do about it. It had

never occurred to him that after twenty three years

of marriage, he was going to have to start working

at it. He thought by now that they would just

"know each other" and it would be, well, easy. By

now she would accept his habits, his faults, his

idiosyncrasies and love him in spite of it all. But

instead he had watched the spark slowly leave her

eyes as the children grew and left and he had

suddenly realized that maybe he wasn't going to be

enough.

He worked a lot and when he did stop for a

moment to consider retirement it was only to think

about the amount of golf he was going to be able to

play. Any trips that were ever discussed always had Jake on the computer looking to see what golf courses were near their destination.

They continued to go out every other Saturday night for dinner and wine at an out of the way, intimate place they had found when they were first married, but conversation now was sparse and, more often than not, he felt she was simply humoring him. When during dinner, he had told her that he had accepted a project that would most likely keep him away for the fall and the winter, and he would be leaving at the end of the week she simply congratulated him and took another sip of wine.

He had hoped that when Karilyne had opened the café it would lift her spirits and give her something to look forward to but instead it had become just one more thing to add to her list of things to do. He couldn't remember the last time he had heard her laugh. He couldn't remember the last time she had sat playfully in his lap and placed her finger over the cleft of his chin or gently touched the new gray at his temples and looked at him with that wistful look, the one that said we've been together since we were kids and now we are growing old together, he loved that look.

She had wanted to take cooking classes together, but he was busy.

She asked him to drive into the city to go to the museums hoping to spark an interest in the art he had once loved but he was busy.

She loved classical music, he loved rock and roll. She loved fairs and he loved fairways.

He measured life by nickels and dimes and she measured it by comings and goings.

She had taken the death of her mother harder than he had expected. It seemed to have changed Karilyne from the strong, capable woman Jake had admired to a morose, vulnerable shell. It had never occurred to him that a large part of their life together had been based upon Karilyne's mother's actions or inactions, approval or disapproval.

Jake Callahan was losing his wife and he had to find a way to get her back.

He knew of only one person who could help make that happen.

Chapter Three

Grace sat in the knotty pine rocking chair that had been hand crafted by her husband, Karilyne's grandfather, and given to her the day they were married. It had sat on the front porch of the cabin he had built through springs, summers and falls and then, inside on a wood planked floor next to the front room fireplace during Midwest winters. She had spent countless hours rocking babies, knitting, reading, and, when time allowed, just thinking as the rhythm of the chair kept time with her heartbeat. It was one of the few possessions she had brought with her to Willow Creek. She felt certain that even though memories of much of her life had begun to fade, the chair would always remind her of her husband, the cabin and love.

She awoke now to see the profile of her only granddaughter staring out of the window at the rows of hedges and wicker benches that had become such a large part of her new life. She looked like her mother and Grace had become aware that, on occasion, she must have mistaken Karilyne for her daughter because Karilyne now began every conversation with "Hi Grandma, it's me, Karilyne." Today she was certain of who was sitting across the room from her and she was certain of something else... Karilyne was in trouble.

Okay, she thought, *make this count.*

"The day you were born you died."

Karilyne's gaze did not shift from the bay window she had been looking through for the past hour as she had waited for her grandmother to awaken. She spoke softly to the air. "Okay, Grandma."

"No, really. Not immediately, but soon... a few hours from the time of your birth... you died." Karilyne turned slowly to face her grandmother, now aware of the tone in Grace's voice and crossed the room to sit next to her. "Tell me."

Grace took Karilyne's strong hand into her tiny,

frail one, her blue eyes clear and sure.

"Your mother awoke to find a nurse standing at the foot of her bed."

Mrs. Wentons third child was born in the fall. The month of October. That glorious month that bridges us from the oppressive heat of summer to the first hint of the winter to come.

At approximately 7:14 p.m., she awoke suddenly in her hospital room. A white capped nurse stood at the foot of the metal crib-style hospital bed in which she lay.

"My baby?"

"She's going to be okay."

"My baby!"

"She is having a little trouble. The doctor is with her now."

Mrs. Wenton rose and quickly shuffled down the pine sol scented corridor to the nursery just in time to see Dr. Marsh gently rubbing the tiny chest of her new daughter while a nurse blew into her once rosy lips.

"Breathe" she whispered, her own breath fogging the single pane window of the nursery.

Her daughter lay still.

"Breathe" she now commanded.

Still no response from the tiny infant as the Dr. continued, his fingers insistent.

"Breathe!" a crescendo that reached a wail and reverberated throughout the 3rd floor of St. John's hospital.

"Karilyne Jane Wenton, this is your mother, now BREATHE!"

And hearing the voice of the woman who had just hours before given her life, Karilyne breathed.

Karilyne sat for a moment, stunned. "Why didn't she ever tell me?"

"Oh, I don't know, dear. Probably didn't want to worry you. I think mostly she didn't want to remember. Easier I think just to put it out of her mind… after all, you did breathe."

"It didn't take me long did It? I guess I was difficult right from the start."

Karilyne closed her eyes and imagined her mother's face, brow knitted.

"I do remember mom shaking her head on occasion and saying *Karilyne, you were born old!* What did she mean by that?"

Grace released Karilyne's hand and placed her small ones in her lap. "There were times when your mother wondered if maybe at the exact time of your "trouble" that the tiny spirit you had been born with had somehow been replaced with an older one."

"I don't understand."

Grace smiled and closed her eyes… remembering. "You were always so practical… so unlike all of the other little girls in the neighborhood. You thought their games were silly and you preferred your books. Your mother worried that you would never have friends."

Karilyne shook her head, "She was right, in a way… I never really had friends. I didn't like parties or, for the most part, social activities. I liked being alone, but I know that had to have been difficult for someone who was homecoming and prom queen! I must have been such a disappointment."

Grace was no longer smiling. "Karilyne Jane! You were never a disappointment! She was your mother and part of a mother's job is to help you find what is best in you… what will make you happy… and to keep you safe. She worried, always, that whatever had taken you for those brief moments in the hospital would return." Grace leaned forward in her wheelchair and looked into Karilyne's worried eyes. "Keeping you safe and giving you the freedom to explore, to spread your wings… to find what would make you happy was a balance she just wasn't sure she could do. So… she chose safe."

Karilyne wanted to hear more, but she knew that this recall had tired Grace. The eyes that had been clear and focused were now beginning to fade. A gentle breeze wafted through the open window, bringing with it the scent of autumn mums. Karilyne breathed deeply and closed her eyes, attempting to process the conversation and the information she had been given. Their weekly talks, when Grace was able, centered around Karilyne's life now… Jake, the kids, the café. This was the first time Karilyne could recall that Grace had spoken of her childhood and she couldn't help but wonder why now? It explained so much! Her mother's constant vigilance. Opportunities that Karilyne did not take due to her mother's "concerns".

No swimming. No climbing. No skating. No tumbling. No living!

It hadn't been control….it had been fear.

The nurse entered the room breaking the silence.

"I'm sorry Karilyne. It is time for Miss Grace to have her medication and a little nap." She crossed the room to adjust Grace's pillows. "She's been up for quite a while now."

"Yes. I know. We had quite a talk."

Karilyne stood to go. "Oh, by the way, Miss Grace has a new doctor and he would like to speak to you for a moment in his office Karilyne."

"A new doctor... why?"

"Well, Doc Moore is retiring and he is introducing all of his patients to new doctors."

Karilyne sighed, "Okay... same office?"

"Yes. At the end of the hall."

Karilyne bent to kiss an already sleeping Grace and entered the hallway. She was not much in the mood for answering a lot of questions. Anything this doctor needed to know he could certainly find in Grace's file or by speaking to the people who cared for her all day on a daily basis.

She was good at meeting and greeting customers at the café. Radiant smile, slightly tilted head, a pat on the arm and the obligatory inquiry into everyone's health. The conversations were limited by time and therefore manageable. Talking with strangers was difficult. She was always guarded and, lately, had given up trying to pretend otherwise.

She would keep this short and sweet.

She knocked lightly on the office door, the brass name plate still reading Dr. Hugh Moore.

The voice on the other side, deeper than Doc Moore's said simply, "Come in."

Chapter Four

Karilyne turned the knob, entered the office, closed the door behind her and turned to extend her hand. She was surprised when her hand was enveloped by two warm hands with long fingers. Karilyne frowned, annoyed by the familiarity. She raised her head and felt the sudden skip of a heartbeat as she looked into the eyes of the man who had once been the boy she had loved in high school. The boy who had left to go to medical school…the boy who had written fervent love letters every day while he was away and the boy whose heart she had broken when she wrote that final letter telling him that she wanted to see other people.

He had never known that there were no other people. Karilyne was simply doing what she felt eventually he would do anyway. How could he possibly be interested in a small town, high school girl when he was surrounded by beautiful, brilliant college girls?

And now here he was. The same laughing blue eyes and crooked smile, holding her hand… her first love.

"Hello Karilyne."

"Hello Kurt."

"I was hoping it was you when I read the last name on your grandmother's chart and then when I saw your name... you know, the spelling, I was certain." The two remained standing, Karilyne's hand still clasped between Kurt's gentle ones. That was Karilyne's strongest memory of Kurt… gentle. He had wanted to be a doctor so he could help, not for the big house or the nice car. She had heard that after graduation he had joined the Peace Corp and was helping people in Africa and she had wanted to be with him, angry at the decision she had made and angrier still when she discovered that he had not had a serious relationship while in school. Her mother kept her updated all during her freshman year at college. Bits and pieces of his whereabouts she gathered from his mother when they saw each other at the grocery store. Karilyne had considered getting in touch with him, but she reasoned that if he wanted to talk to her he would certainly know how to find her. She hadn't thought of being with anyone else until the night she met Jake.

Kurt released her hand and motioned to a small, vinyl office chair. "I'm sorry. Please, have a seat." Karilyne hesitated for a moment, but then accepted his offer... after all it was likely that he only wanted some information on Grace. They sat opposite each other, smiling over Kurt's desk, bare, except for a small laptop and a photograph of a pretty, freckled, redhead flanked by two smiling, smaller versions, one with a lavender ribbon in her hair, the other, green.

"Your family?"

"Yes" Kurt's eyes rested for a moment on the family

photograph. Not a formal portrait, but a snapshot taken someplace warm and sunny.

"They're beautiful."

Kurt cleared his throat and looked back at the girl he had known so many years ago. "Thank you."

Silence permeated the room as they both tried to think of something to say.

Karilyne spoke first. "I'm sorry, Kurt. I would like to get caught up, but I really have to get to work. Was there something you needed to know about Grace?" The reason Karilyne still believed she had been summoned to his office.

Kurt smiled sheepishly. "No. I've read her chart. I don't need any information now, I just wanted to see you, but I don't want to hold you up."

Kurt stood and Karilyne joined him.

"It was good to see you." Karilyne opened the door to go.

Kurt hesitated for only a moment. "Karilyne, maybe next time you come to visit, we could spend a little more time catching up… go for a walk."

Karilyne smiled and relaxed… suddenly aware of the tension across her shoulders, "I would like that. I'll be back on Thursday, what time do you take lunch?"

Kurt shoved his hands deep into his jean pockets and cocked his head "Any time you get here, Karly."

Karilyne laughed, "You were the only one that ever called me Karly! It used to drive my mother *crazy!*"

Kurt's smile widened to a grin, "I remember… that's why I always made sure to ask for Karly when I called your house."

"You only got away with it because she liked you so much."

"Your mother had very good taste!"

They had come to the end of the hall and arrived at the exit door. Kurt punched a series of numbers into the security keypad and attempted the door. As the alarm sounded a nurse peered through the office glass. Kurt waved and the alarm stopped. "Sorry…

I'm new here." Karilyne laughed. "Just remember…

the date changes every day to match the current

day and then Willow spelled backwards."

Karilyne entered the code and opened the door.

"See… nothing to it."

Kurt shook his head, "Might be easier just to climb

in and out of my window every day." *The way I*

used to climb in and out of yours.

Kurt held the door and as Karilyne began to walk

through the parking lot she remembered their lunch

date. She turned to walk back but found that Kurt

was still standing at the door watching her. She

blushed and hoped that she was far enough away

that he couldn't see it. She cupped her mouth and

called back "1:30 sharp… I'll bring the food." Kurt

nodded, waved and walked back into the building.

A gust of wind lifted Karilyne's skirt and scattered

snowflakes across her cheeks and into her hair. She

giggled and tilted her head back. The first snow of

the season… one of her favorite days… this had to be a sign!

She practically skipped to her car and slid into the driver's seat. She took one last look back at the front doors of Willow Creek and caught a glimpse of her reflection in the car's window. Was she actually smiling? *Oh my god! What are you doing? He's married. You're married.* She started the car and rifled through the glove box for a pair of last winter's gloves. As she slid the soft cashmere over her left hand, she realized she wasn't wearing her wedding ring. She had a habit of removing it anytime that she helped Jaclyn mix the bread doughs. *I left it on the counter.* She realized that she hadn't mentioned Jake and wondered if Kurt had taken note of her bare left hand. *Is that why he asked me to have lunch… he doesn't know I'm married or he thinks I'm divorced… or he doesn't care either way.*

Serendipity: the accidental discovery of something pleasant.

Stop over thinking this Karilyne. He's just an old friend from high school and, besides, I can't think of anyone else I would rather have caring for Grace.

The ride back to the café was a pleasant one and for the first time in a long time, Karilyne saw a small light at the end of a shortening tunnel.

Chapter Five

Patricia scarcely noticed the beautiful fall leaves that lined the narrow lane that would lead her sight unseen to her new home and new life. The wood paneled station wagon groaned under the weight of her old life. Clothing, books, music, odds and ends of furniture that she couldn't leave behind.

"I am sorry." The old man had told her. "I am afraid the radio doesn't work anymore."

But that was okay with Patricia... she needed the silence. Mile after mile of quiet. Occasionally she sang softly to herself the songs they used to sing together until the break in her voice made her aware of the tears that blurred the signs that lined the highway.

For the most part, she had taken her time. There was no rush. She had transferred the money to the owner and he had mailed her the deed so the house would be waiting regardless of when she arrived.

She stopped at quaint shops along the way and purchased small items she thought she might need for the house. Small cafes beckoned with homemade treats which she ate in her car unable to stand the sound of happy conversations.

The last day of her trip she set out determined to make her destination while there would still be light. She took the exit marked ALLERT VILLAGE and followed the directions given to her by the home's previous owner. She passed through the village, drove approximately four miles and then turned onto an unpaved dirt road. A small wooden sign read Patchwork Farm.

The road took a slight bend and the car stopped at a gate. Patricia sat for a moment her head resting on the steering wheel. She took a deep breath, stepped out of the car and stretched, her arms extended towards the late afternoon sun. The gate was latched with a single hook and, when unlatched, swung open easily and came to rest against a rugged, large planked fence. The house appeared to be about a ½ mile from the fence. The sun sat just above a brick chimney, casting a beautiful, inviting golden glow that spilled onto the front porch. A lone rocking chair rocked gently as an autumn breeze rustled the leaves and blew Patricia's soft, dark hair across her face.

She closed her eyes and listened.

Honking from a flock of geese broke the silence, but only for a moment and then… nothing.

Absolutely nothing.

The house was empty except for a few pieces of furniture that Patricia had requested and the owner had agreed to leave. A bed and chest of drawers in the bedroom. A kitchen table with two chairs, refrigerator and stove that had been in the house since the mid-fifties, but were "still in excellent condition", he had explained, remained in the kitchen. Patricia looked through the kitchen window. A free standing clothes line stood not far from the back porch. A tire swing hung from a towering oak and tomato baskets, twine and poles lay neatly stacked just outside of what appeared to be a gardening shed.

She carried in only what she needed for now. Bedding, candles and a cooler that held enough food to get her through a day or two. She cut the string that held the only chair she had brought with her, a rocker, and placed it in the living room just in front of the red, brick fireplace. She built a small fire with the wood she retrieved from the back porch and newspaper left in a basket under the front room window.

She placed a bottle of wine and a glass next to the chair and made one last trip to the car. She set the box gently on the floor, opened it and removed the bath towels that had ensured a trip free of breakage. She lifted the urn from its cradle of foam and, using one of the towels, wiped away the small amount of dust that had managed to seep inside the box. She held it in her arms for a moment and then placed it on the mantel. She sat in the chair and rocked, the only sound was the crackle of the firewood. After several minutes, Patricia knelt again next to the box. Her hands trembled as she removed the second urn. A much smaller one, blue with butterflies she had hand painted herself. She cradled it for a moment before placing it next to the larger one. She poured a glass of wine, lifted it and, in the silence whispered "welcome home."

Chapter Six

Frankie walked softly down the hallway, careful not to waken a sleeping Angie Cappelli. He knew that she never expected to find him there after one of their alcohol fueled hookups but he also knew that she was forever hopeful. He pulled a large cable knit sweater over his tousled hair and retrieved his boots from the hall before slipping out the front door. He stretched and allowed normal breathing to begin, his deep exhale becoming a moist gray cloud in the chilly autumn air. A gust of wind lifted the leaves off of the top of a newly raked pile and carried them down Logan lane, playfully scattering them across freshly manicured lawns.

Frankie slowly opened the door to his van, trying to minimize the creak that had only recently begun. He slid into the driver's seat, started the van and jumped at the radio's volume. He quickly reached for the knob and turned it off. He adjusted the rear view mirror towards him and ran his fingers through the unruly black curls. He sat for a minute studying his reflection and wondering when exactly the lines that now framed his dark brown eyes had appeared. He had been forced to admit that the crowd that now gathered at The Alley seemed to be getting younger and that he and Angie had been two of the oldest people there. He wasn't exactly sure when that had happened either and may not have noticed until the new bartender who appeared to be about sixteen called him sir when he had ordered their drinks.

Daily work on the farm kept Frankie's muscular arms and shoulders defined and his waist whittled. He felt every bit as strong now as he had when he was a fullback on the high school football team. Except maybe his knees at the end of the day... maybe his back first thing in the morning.

He was the last of the old gang to spend his

weekends at the old haunts with new names… the rest of them had traded in places like the Alley and girls like Angie for the demands of domesticity. For a while they had continued to gather at Louie's for a beer or two, but Frankie wasn't someone that the "wives" wanted their husbands to be around and little by little they had all come up with one lame excuse after another until one Friday night Frankie realized that the only familiar face in the mirrored bar back was his own.

Still… he was happy… wasn't he?

He placed the mirror in the correct position and backed down the drive. He drove through the middle of the quiet village… a lull before the buzz of daily life began. He passed St. James and slowed as he approached the village square. He had promised himself that as soon as his vineyards were doing well enough to warrant it, he would call Mr. Norman about the old, empty building next to the antique shop and begin selling bottles of his wines.

The place had been closed up for about fifteen years and he had no reason to believe it would be any different until he was ready to use it but this morning it appeared that someone else was interested in it. A slim woman with beautiful auburn hair was placing a key into the door knob. Frankie pulled over and began to park the van but after catching a glimpse of the tired face that looked back at him from the side view mirror, he decided this wasn't the way he wanted to present himself to his newest conquest. He would find out soon enough who she was and what she was doing in Mr. Norman's building.

He started the van and checked his watch… he had just enough time to help Rose get the kids off to school before beginning the work that would protect his crops through the winter.

Chapter Seven

"Remember…" that's what Grace had said to Jake
the afternoon he left town. He had wanted to tell
her personally that he was leaving for business that
he still loved Karilyne with all his heart but he
wasn't sure loving her was enough. He knew that
Grace knew Karilyne better than anyone…better
than he did…better than the mother she longed for
and, yes, even better than Karilyne herself.
Grace listened to all Jake had to say and smiled.
"Remember, Jake."
"Remember what, Grace?" Jake was puzzled. Was
there something Grace remembered that he had
forgotten?
"You are making this too hard. Granted, Karilyne is
not an easy woman. She expects a lot from herself
and those around her."
Jake smiled "I know… it was always one of the

things I loved about her... never settling. But now there is more to it. Something is gone. It's as though she has just realized that she spent a lifetime building a life she doesn't want. Grace, we used to have fun. Oh, I know that sounds trite and I don't mean for it to. We used to laugh together. We talked... we made plans." Jake paused for a moment running his fingers through his thick, salt and pepper hair.

He continued. "She used to know who she was. Who we were. And when the days got long and tough and I sometimes wondered who I was, at the end of the day I always found myself in Karilyne's eyes. It was more than happy, it was more than contentment... it was pure joy. Karilyne used to have joy."

Grace fingered the edge of the crocheted blanket that covered her lap. "It can't have gone far. You're going to have to find it. Remember what gave her joy. Remember what made you love her and why and, even more importantly, what made her love you."

Jake shook his head. "That sounds easy, but life gets a little complicated. We change, we grow, and we become different people."

"Baloney!"

Jake smiled. He knew even as he was saying it that Grace would disagree.

"Karilyne is searching, Jake."

"For what?" exasperation now edging into Jake's tired voice.

"I'm not sure. Neither is Karilyne. Something from her past that will assure her that she is who she thought she was all along. We begin to lose ourselves when we lose the ones we love. Little snippets of our lives that we try desperately to hang on to... the way someone's voice sounds, a certain look at any given moment, the shape of a hand. As time erases those, we feel ourselves being erased as well. She lost her father when she was so young, then, of course, her mother just when she was reaching a stage in her life when she knew the questions that she wanted to ask and now, well, she's losing me."

Jake knew all of this to be true… he just wasn't sure what to do about it.

"Any advice Grace?"

Grace looked into the beautiful face of the only man that had ever been right for Karilyne, the only man who would forever be right for Karilyne. "Don't listen to what anyone else has to say. Don't ask for and don't take the advice of your buddies, your pals, your co-workers or do-gooders. None of them know your hearts."

Jake nodded. "I hope maybe this business trip will help… maybe some time to herself will give her some of the answers she is looking for. You know what they say "absence makes the heart grow fonder!"

Grace shook her head, "Never worked for me… I

hated every second that Karilyne's grandfather was gone, no matter the reason and I now spend my days counting the seconds until I can be with him again."

Jake rested his hands on Grace's hands… his voice soft and low, "I want that."

"Then go and find it, Jake."

Jake stood and stretched, retrieving his coat and satchel from the bay window sill, "They don't tell you about all of this stuff when you get married, do they?"

Grace laughed, "No… I suppose none of us would get married if we knew from the beginning how much work it takes!" Jake leaned over to kiss a tired Grace. She looked again into Jakes eyes… feeling her own growing heavy and placed her hand on his cheek, "too bad someone hasn't written a book with all the answers."

Jake smiled, "Yeah… that would be great… a book!"

Jake sat in the parking lot thinking about their conversation. *Remember. Karilyne's joy. Find it. A book.* Jake smiled, maybe he would write a book when this was all over with, a marriage manual starting from the wedding day through planning a house, having kids, middle age... all of it. He started the car and checked the rearview mirror before backing up. The leaves at Willow Brook were breathtaking in their fall colors just like the leaves had been on their wedding day.

Jake laughed out loud... *A book. Wait...of course there's a book!*

Jake delayed his trip for a couple of hours. Long enough to return home after he was certain Karilyne was gone. He carefully removed the stained bibs, blankets and baby books from the cedar chest Karilyne's mother had given her when Jillianne had been born, lifted the scrapbook and their wedding album from the bottom, replaced everything just as he had found it, except for the books and the album. Those he placed carefully into a small canvas satchel and left.

As he backed down the drive, he paused to look at the house, the home they had created together. He couldn't lose it. He couldn't lose her. Somewhere in the pages of the books that lay on the seat beside him he would remember. Through Karilyne's memories, the "snippets" of their life, he would find her joy.

Winter

Chapter Eight

The snow that had tickled Karilyne's nose and dusted her windshield at Willow Creek slowly turned into the first real snow of the season. Large, wet flakes clung to the wrought iron fence that surrounded St. James' church and blew in crystalline circles down Main Street. Children built snowmen and the local grocer gave them carrot sticks to complete their frosty creations.

Suicide hill once again became treacherous for cars and school buses and an icy haven for speeding sleds when frazzled mothers shooed stranded children outside while the schools were closed. Losing power was an inevitable part of country living and one bright young entrepreneur set up a candle and flashlight stand on the corner of Main and Elm St. and did quite well. Karilyne kept him supplied with hot chocolate and sugar cookies. The small downtown shops bustled with shoppers who were willing to spend a bit more for locally crafted baskets, gift boxes, quilts and scarves simply to be able to spend the day in the pastoral village away from the hustle and bustle of the city. The majority of these shoppers would be unable to resist a stop at Karilyne's as the door would open briefly and the smell of winter warmth wafted through the crisp December air. Nostrils flared and eyelashes fluttered and deep *Ahhhs!* were heard as telltale stomachs insisted upon a bowl of steaming soup followed with a hand painted china dessert plate overflowing with one of Jaclyn's desserts.

The holidays were in full swing and Karilyne couldn't be sure whether the warmth in the café came from the ovens perpetual heat or from Jaclyn's perpetual cheer. It didn't matter… everyone left with full bellies and full hearts.

French onion, wild rice with mushroom and broccoli with cheese were, of course, standard fare, but to those who paid attention to the daily chalk board they would find a daily specialty such as Sausage with black bean, Hungarian pork goulash with fresh egg noodles, Minestrone with white beans and pasta and Split pea with smoked ham and fresh thyme. Date nut, corn and beer breads were baked daily and carefully paired with each bowl.

And the desserts. Oh my! The desserts.

Jaclyn made Buche du Noel and beautiful little spice cakes dipped in powdered sugar, wrapped in cellophane and tied with red and green ribbons. Cinnamon rolls, sugar cookies, fudge and divinity were displayed on lace doilies in the glass case just below the cash register and there wasn't a customer who walked out empty handed!

The bell above the door rang sweetly and often for the entire holiday so much so that Karilyne became sick of hearing "Every time a bell rings an angel gets its wings".

"Jingle bells, jingle bells, jingle all the way" Jaclyn's

sweet voice had been a virtual Christmas album since the day after Thanksgiving. She sang while she mixed, baked, frosted and dusted. She hummed while she chopped, diced, sautéed and stirred. Karilyne didn't see any way that Jaclyn could have more energy than she had on a daily basis but she had been wrong. The first week in December, Jaclyn resembled a windup doll whose key was stuck on high. Her Christmas spirit was contagious to not only those people who chose the café for a little taste of the holidays but, it seemed, to the entire village… to all but Karilyne. In the midst of all of the Christmas cheer, Karilyne's gloom pervaded. Jillianne had called from school to ask… to tell… Karilyne that she wanted to spend Christmas in France. The school's madrigal group had been learning French Christmas carols and they were invited to perform in Paris during the holidays. Her professor had made arrangements for them to stay with host families. "It won't cost much… just a few meals and a little shopping!" her voice pleading.

Karilyne closed her eyes, remembering the lights, the cafes, the shops and the few, small snowflakes that had floated through the crisp Parisian air. The locals shook their heads, "It is rare to have snow in Paris." Karilyne just smiled, knowing Mother Nature had given her a Holiday gift.

"Your professor is right. Your father and I spent a Christmas in Paris... you should go."

"Thanks mom! I will miss you and dad, but on the up side, I will be able to have Christmas dinner with Josh!"

She hadn't told the kids that Jake had been gone for over a month and might be gone much longer. As far as they were concerned, it was business as usual... it had always been necessary for their father to leave for short periods of time on special projects but he was always home for the holidays. *No matter what.*

All of the customers were gone and a steady snow

had begun to fall. Karilyne turned the front door sign to CLOSED and scooted one of the rockers closer to the window. She dimmed the lights and covered her lap with one of the quilts that Mrs. Watson, Jaclyn's neighbor, had made for them. She heard Jaclyn's voice and called to her. "Jaclyn… don't worry about cleaning up, I'll get it, I'm sure you have things to do… shopping or decorating."

"Not really. Here." Jaclyn handed Karilyne a champagne flute filled with pink bubbles and scooted a second rocker next to Karilyne. Karilyne lifted the flute towards the white lights that surrounded the window and watched the bubbles sparkle and rise to the top of the glass "What is this?"

"This is a very special drink that my mother made only during the holidays. I had forgotten about it until I was in the city and saw a bottle of the liqueur she used. I've been saving it until the first real snow. "

Karilyne once again had to remind herself that Jaclyn was a twenty four year old woman and certainly old enough to drink "I didn't know you drank!"

Jaclyn winked, lowered her voice, and held her glass up, "Oh, there is much you don't know about me!"

Karilyne's eyes widened "Really!?"

Jaclyn giggled "No... not really."

The two women laughed and clinked their glasses together. "Merry Christmas!"

They sat in silence for a bit watching the snow fall and sipping the raspberry flavored champagne.

Jaclyn cleared her throat, knowing the answer to the question before she asked, "Did you get your Christmas tree up?"

Karilyne took another sip and sat back in her rocker, "I didn't see much point in it this year. The kids will be in Paris and..."

"Wait... what? I knew Josh was there, but Jillianne?"

Karilyne closed her eyes and pictured her children in sweaters and stocking caps lobbing carefully packed snowballs at each other in their back yard during the holiday school breaks. "I forgot to mention it. Jilli called and said she was going with the madrigal group from school. Jake says he will be here, but I've seen the weather report and it doesn't look good, it just didn't seem worth all the trouble. Once he's gone it would only remind me that I'm alone."

Jaclyn shook her head. "I'm alone."

"I'm sorry Jaclyn… I didn't think… so why do you do it? Why do you go through all the time, trouble and ultimate mess when you are the only one there?"

Jaclyn shrugged, her cheeks flushed from the champagne.

"Well, I guess because a Christmas tree, for me, represents memories, some happy some sad, and hope. When I put the tree up I am thankful for

68

another year, and especially this year when I found the café. Being able to do what I love to do in the village that I care so much about means the world to me. I am grateful that I got to spend some time with my dad before he died. I am grateful even for those long, lonely years in Chicago... they taught me how much I love my home and the people who live here."

Jaclyn placed her long, slender fingers over Karilyne's, "I am grateful for you."

Karilyne smiled, "I wish I had your attitude. I wish I could find some Christmas cheer."

"Well, I know of a place where you could certainly *give* some Christmas cheer and you never know... you might just find some."

"Really... where is this magical place?"

"The annual St. James Christmas dinner... we could use the extra pair of hands!"

Karilyne began a weak protest, "I don't know... Christmas eve. I'll probably just stay home and..."

Jaclyn was already on her feet and headed towards the kitchen with the empty flutes and she wasn't going to take no for an answer. "If Jake gets home wonderful! If he doesn't I will not allow you to sit at home alone and brood. You can just as easily brood while you serve ham and yams."

Karilyne didn't have the energy to argue, besides, the champagne had softened her a little bit and the snow, well, the snow always made her happy.

Christmas eve... the kids will be dining in Paris, Jake in some luxury hotel suite and I will be at St. James spooning out lumpy mashed potatoes... humbug!!

Chapter Nine

Jake's bare feet formed a trail of plush imprints in the hotel carpeting that ran the length of the suite's living room. The first frost that had painted beautiful frozen frescoes across the balcony doors had quickly become a relentless torrent of snow and ice... a winter war waged against the taxicabs and airports... and Christmas.

He had promised Karilyne that he would be home... *no matter what* and now he was faced with the reality of what a winter storm meant in North Dakota. He knew he would have to call her. It would take a miracle to halt the heavy snow and the weather channel gave no such indication that a miracle was imminent.

They had never spent a Christmas apart. First, just the two of them and then before they knew it, the four of them. Always together for the holidays... *no matter what*. There were always extras of course, family, friends and dates, but it boiled down to the four of them, Karilyne, Jake, Jillianne and Joshua. Now it looked like he would be stuck in Fargo, the kids in Paris and, he feared, Karilyne would be frozen to the Allert Village bench!

He stopped pacing long enough to hit speed dial to the airport and waited for the answer he knew he would receive… all flights cancelled.

Dammit!! I should have gone two days ago, before all of this mess started. I promised her I would be there. He collapsed into the overstuffed chair he had placed in front of one of the large panes of glass that had provided breathtaking views for the last few months and sighed. He laid his head against the curved back of the chair and allowed the phone to drop to the floor. He closed his eyes and smiled, picturing their holiday home. The wreaths, the flocking, the tree… not this year… he knew without the kids, Karilyne wouldn't get a tree. There would be no decorating, no baking, no long walks through the fresh snow followed by mugs of mulled wine,

snuggling in front of the fireplace he had designed

and built brick by brick.

He stretched long fingers to retrieve the phone,

there was no point in putting it off any longer. He

dialed and waited for Karilyne to answer.

For just a second Karilyne thought maybe Jake was

calling to say he was on his way home but she knew

better. She muted the weather channel, wrapped an

afghan around her shoulders and answered.

"Hello."

Jake's heart sank… the tone in just her hello said it

all… she knew he wasn't coming.

"Hey babe" silence on the other end. "I guess

you've seen the weather report. I'm sorry Karilyne."

Karilyne sighed, her eyes tearing "It's… it's okay."

She was determined that he not hear the tears

through her voice. "You can't control the weather."

"That's true, but I could have planned a little

better… I didn't realize how bad things were gonna

get."

Karilyne walked slowly through the house, stopping at the breakfast nook bay windows to watch a doe and her fawn nibbling at the snow covered tree branches.

"It's hard to believe that there is a place that gets snowier and colder than it gets here!"

Jake laughed, "I know! You would have to see it to really believe it. They have managed to keep the power on... hey, how bout there? Do you have power?"

Karilyne placed the tea kettle onto the stove, flipped the burner to high and dropped a tea bag into a music note covered mug. "Yes... no problems here. Of course you know talking about it has probably jinxed me... it will inevitably go out the minute we hang up."

"Don't say that! You should probably get somebody to carry the generator in just in case."

Karilyne smiled, "I will but don't worry, I have

plenty of firewood, blankets and wine!"

"That's my girl! Of course, some of the best times we ever had with the kids were during power outages... playing board games and eating lots of junk!"

"I remember some pretty good power outages before the kids."

Jake closed his eyes and pictured Karilyne. She would be in plaid, flannel pants and one of his sweatshirts, her hair falling over her shoulders, sipping tea from her music mug. "Any gifts under the tree?"

Karilyne stirred a spoonful of honey into her tea and looked at the empty living room corner. "Just a few."

"Truth?"

Karilyne sighed, "The truth is that I have a couple of gifts wrapped and sitting next to a poinsettia on the dining room table."

"No tree?"

"No… no tree. We always did that as a family and this year… I just didn't want to do it alone."

Jake poured a splash of scotch over the ice in a rocks glass. "I am sorry, Karilyne."

"I know… any end in sight?"

"No… not for this storm" Jake took a drink, "or for this project."

Karilyne's heart sank. Even if the snow stopped, he would stay for the duration of the project. It was becoming more and more evident that this grand building in North Dakota… his work… was more important than Christmas. More important than their life. More important than Karilyne.

"I have a call ringing on the other line," Karilyne lied. "I have to go."

Jake knew there was no other call. He knew that it was just Karilyne's way of saying that there was no further need for conversation… she had heard all she needed to. "OK… I'll call you tomorrow night?"

Karilyne's tears had begun before she could reply

"Christmas eve… it's not as though I have any plans."

She ended the call before Jake could respond. She felt a twinge of guilt making him feel bad, if, in fact he did. She paused in front of the hallway mirror. Her eyes swollen and red, tears streaming down her cheeks. *Boy you are really feeling sorry for yourself, aren't you? Poor Karilyne. Nobody loves me, everybody hates me think I'll go eat…* she stopped and straightened, her hands on her hips she took a deep breath of resolve. *Ham and yams…I'm going to eat ham and yams!*

She wiped her tears, blew her nose and dialed Jaclyn's number.

Chapter ten

Although the original plan had been to meet at St. James "Wear something Christmasy" had been her instructions, Jaclyn phoned and asked that Karilyne come to her house before they go to the dinner and it occurred to Karilyne that she had never been to Jaclyn's home. She was familiar with the little yellow bungalow and had driven past it dozens of times, but she had never actually stopped, even on those days when she knew Jaclyn would have been home. She knew that Jaclyn wanted her to see her Christmas tree hoping that it would put Karilyne in a holiday mood and the pep talk she had given herself while wrapping the few gifts she had purchased included a joyful response to Jaclyn's efforts.

She drove slowly over the snow covered country roads looking from side to side for the fawn that she had seen nibbling on the apple tree bark. Where there were little deer there would be big deer

foraging for food beneath the fresh snow before

settling in for the night and all of them were

oblivious to the occasional car as they leapt across

the roads that ran between the fields. The air was

crisp and still... perfect sledding weather for the

holiday revelers... a beautiful, brief, winter

wonderland before the inevitable below zero temps

and gale force winds that would soon besiege the

village.

The lights from the village were visible from even a

mile away and Karilyne felt a shiver of holiday

excitement. Main Street was breathtaking. The

large pine that stood year round in the village

square was bedecked with the ornaments

handmade by the scout troops, the ladies auxiliary

and the St. James bible club. They would remain on

the tree until January 3rd when they would be

removed and auctioned off to raise money for the

following year's veterans' Christmas baskets.

Mr. Vandyke had Molly hooked to an antique sleigh equipped with Mrs. Watsons lap quilts and home baked gingerbread men. The same young salesman who had made good use of the corner selling flashlights and candles at the beginning of November had now recruited his father and the two were selling steaming cups of hot chocolate or spiced wine... a perfect accompaniment to a brisk sleigh ride through the village to see the lights and decorations.

The nativity scene that stood on the front lawn of St. James had been a gift from Jake, built in his now unused workshop. Karilyne's eyes brimmed with tears and she scolded herself for being sentimental. She was going to enjoy herself this evening... *no matter what!*

She continued through town and pulled into Jaclyn's driveway. It was what she had expected... Santa and the reindeer in perpetual playful flight from Jaclyn's yard. The front windows wrapped in garland and twinkling white lights… an overly

large wreath decorated by Girl Scout Troop 162

hung on the front door, slightly overlapping the

door's frame. Karilyne smiled at the innocence…

the pure joy that Jaclyn brought to everything she

did. She lifted the carefully wrapped package from

the front seat and walked through the snow to

Jaclyn's porch. Before she could knock, Jaclyn was

there opening the door, grabbing Karilyne's arm…

pulling her into the house.

"Merry Christmas! Come in!"

Karilyne laughed, "Merry Christmas to you!!"

If the outside of the house had been exactly what

Karilyne had expected the inside was nothing like

what she had expected. None of the Santa

gaudiness… no plastic elves or oversized candy

canes, but rather the absolute beauty of the season.

A simple nativity on the dining room table. Framed

photos of Christmas' past on the walls. Fragrant

garland with wisps of colored ribbon flowed across

the mantel and, just above the hearth… three stockings.

The tree was decorated with Jaclyn's handmade ornaments… some obviously from her childhood, but the majority from more recent years… meticulously molded and colored holly berries, birds and, of course, Jaclyn's beloved butterflies. Who else would put butterflies on a Christmas tree?

"It's beautiful Jaclyn."

"You really think so Karilyne? I wanted you to like it."

"I do… very much… it's perfect."

Jaclyn knelt at the base of the tree and began to rummage through the various packages, careful not to tear the hand stamped paper she had created for each one. "Here it is!"

She stood and handed Karilyne a single, rectangular package. "This one has your name on it."

Karilyne smiled, "and this one has yours on it!"

The two women sat on the couch, feeling the

packages for clues of their contents... savoring the

moment of the first Christmas gift.

Jaclyn broke the silence, "You first Karilyne...

please."

Karilyne turned the package over and began

untying the colored twine. "The wrapping is so

beautiful I don't want to tear it."

Jaclyn beamed and clutched her gift to her chest...

her childlike anticipation palpable.

The wrapping off and laid to one side, Karilyne

turned over what was obviously a picture frame.

Secured inside the frame under a piece of glass was

an exact replica of Karilyne's Korner... perfectly

cross-stitched. The brick walls, the garden, the

windows... complete with a variety of pastries, the

bell over the door and the tables set with the

antique china. She gasped as tears began to form at

the corners of her eyes, "Jaclyn... it's... it... I don't

have the words. I am overwhelmed with not only

the beauty of the work but your thoughtfulness. It is

incredible and I will cherish it… and you."

"Please, open yours. I can promise you one thing…
it doesn't compare to this!!"

"Karilyne, if you chose it for me, I am sure I will
love it!"

And she did. The frame was old and very fragile. A
beautiful woman wearing a flowing pink organza
gown seated at a mirrored vanity had been
carefully painted on a thin pane of glass. A piece of
foil placed behind the glass made the gown and
mirror appear to shimmer.

"It is from the Chicago's world fair. My
grandmother purchased it and gave it to me when I
was in my teens. As you can see by the description
on the back, the process was called the Butterfly
Wings effect. It is the combination of painting
directly onto the glass and the patterned foil placed
behind that make it so unique. I have held onto it all
these years waiting…"

"To give it to Jillianne?"

Karilyne smiled and shook her head. "No… I don't think so. I mean probably but I never did and, now, I think I know why."

Jaclyn sat quietly for a moment, her fingertips tracing the gown's outline, "Do you think you were saving it for me?"

Karilyne wrapped her arm around Jaclyn's small shoulders, "Yes… I think so."

At that moment, both women knew that somehow their meeting had been no accident and that their time together at the café had been about more than soup and chocolate.

Jaclyn smiled, "Like you and me."

"Like me and you?"

"Your soups and my cakes… unique, our very own Butterfly effect!"

The clock on the mantel chimed reminding them that they had somewhere they needed to be.

"Oh my gosh! We had better get going or Father O'Brien is going to be up to his elbows in parishioners and potatoes."

Kurt had been recruited by one of the nurses at Willow Creek to help at St. James. He thought it would be best to spend Christmas eve at home with his girls but when he explained that St. James was serving food to people who may not have a place to go on Christmas Eve or maybe too old to cook, his daughters did not hesitate… they would do whatever would help and they wanted to bake cookies to contribute to the dessert table. *Dad, everybody should have a sugar cookie on Christmas!!* They spent three days mixing, rolling, cutting, baking and decorating the cookies their mother had taught them to make and when all was said and done, they had a little more than 200 cookies to deliver.

The parking lot at St. James was already filling rapidly and the spots closest to the kitchen entrance were taken. Although the cookies could have easily fit into two foil roasting pans, the girls had painstakingly decorated each one and placed them in between layers of parchment paper in a total of six pans making it impossible for Kurt to carry them all at once. He had been given strict instructions not to allow a single cookie to get "smooshed or cracked!" He circled the lot once, hoping that maybe someone was simply dropping off a covered dish and leaving but no such luck. He chose a spot at the far end of the lot being certain to leave any closer spots for those people who needed them and resigned himself to making several trips with the cookie filled foil pans.

As he leaned into the trunk to retrieve the first two pans a car pulled into the adjacent spot and a familiar voice called, "Hey handsome!" Kurt quickly backed out of the trunk's interior bumping his head on the door as the top pan began to slide precariously towards the parking lot.

Karilyne caught the cookies… laughing. "That was

close!"

Jaclyn had walked past the couple and was already holding two pans.

"Look at this… Christmas eve and two angels appear out of nowhere to help me carry cookies!"

"At your service, sir, and we had better pick up the pace before we end up with dish duty."

The three began the walk through the lot as a light snow began to fall. Jaclyn squealed "Perfect!!" Karilyne and Kurt glanced at each other. "I'm sorry… I didn't introduce you… Kurt this is Jaclyn… Jaclyn, Kurt. Ok Jaclyn… hit it!"

We wish you a merry Christmas, we wish you a merry Christmas "Everybody!!" *We wish you a merry Christmas….*

Frankie was at the back door of the church unloading large roasters filled with the vegetables he had prepared for the dinner, potatoes, carrots, turnips and butternut squash when the cheerful trio walked past him. He barely glanced away from the task at hand, but then did a double take when he thought he recognized the beautiful woman with the long auburn hair. He carried in the last pan and began to rummage through the kitchen drawers for serving spoons, keeping one eye and both ears in Karilyne's direction.

Father O'Brien greeted his volunteers, "Ah! Here you are. Thank you for helping us out this year Kurt, Jaclyn and so good to see you here, Karilyne."

Karilyne. Karilyne. The name didn't ring a bell, but Frankie felt certain he knew her from somewhere. It wasn't from any of the bars or clubs and she hadn't been to the farm... he would have remembered that. *Karilyne.* He checked his watch. He wanted to stay and find out more, but he needed to assemble the toys that Rose had bought for the kids and get them under the tree. He would have to wait until he came back for the pans and ask Father O'Brien, casually, of course, who the redhead was who had helped.

Karilyne smiled as she wrapped the oversized apron strings around her waist, "Happy to be here Father... now if you will just hand me a spoon and show me my station on the serving line..."

Father O'Brien shook his head, "There is no serving line. Tonight, you will be waiting on the tables."

"Oh... I'm sorry, I thought it was served buffet style."

"Keep in mind Karilyne that most of the people here tonight cannot afford to go to restaurants... they stand in line at soup lines, they stand in line at food pantries... they stand in line at welfare offices and clinics. So tonight, we will wait on them, just as Jesus did for his disciples. Tonight we will let them know that no matter their circumstances, *they* will matter.... they are loved. You see that we have several veterans here, many disabled... proud men who certainly would not balk at walking through a food line and balancing a plate of food back to a table... but not tonight, tonight we are going to show them how much we appreciate their sacrifice." Father O'Brien paused as he looked over the assembled diners. "And as we place a plate in front of each soul, we smile and bless them and we thank God for all that we have and remind ourselves that it is only through his grace that, tonight, we are the servers and not those waiting to be served."

Dinner passed quickly and just as father O'brien had said, Karilyne met people that she would never have met during her daily life. Some of them from the village and many of them from the city who boarded buses just to be able to have Christmas Eve dinner at St. James.

The dinner plates were stacked in the deep kitchen sinks and Karilyne was placing desserts on one of the rolling carts when Father O'Brien placed his hand on her shoulder. "Karilyne, you've worked hard this evening… time for a break, there is someone I want you to meet." The priest chose two plates with a small variety of desserts and handed them to Karilyne. "Follow me."

The majority of the diners was mingling or had moved into the small chapel where the junior choir was leading them in Christmas carols. Karilyne followed Father O'brien to a table in the back of the dining room where a woman sat alone. "Ruth, this is Karilyne… I told her it was time for a break and what's a break without dessert!" Ruth smiled and scooted a chair out for Karilyne.

Karilyne sat, placed the plates on the table and began the conversation by asking the same question she had asked dozens of times throughout the evening "How was your dinner?"

Ruth bit the head off of a sugar Santa and covered her mouth, "It was delicious… it always is."

"You've had this dinner before?"

Ruth nodded, "Yes, every year for the last six years. I always brought my mother… this was her parish."

"*Was* her parish?"

Ruth sighed and laid the cookie on the table. "Yes...
she died just before Thanksgiving this year."
Suddenly Karilyne realized the reason for the
meeting, Father O'Brien thought she would be able
to help this woman with her grief. He didn't know
that she hadn't even handled her own grief. He
didn't know that since her mother's death, she
questioned who she was... what her life meant. But
mostly, he couldn't possibly realize that she no
longer believed... that her faith had died with her
mother.

"I'm so sorry. I know how you must feel, I lost my
mother a little over a year ago."

"Thank you and I'm sorry for your loss as well."
Karilyne took a bite from a mini cheesecake and
wondered what to say next. *What words of wisdom do
I have to offer!?* "Do you live here in the village?"
Ruth shook her head, "No. My parents were from
the village, but moved to the city when they
married. I had been working in St. Louis but when

my father died, and then mom got sick, I moved back to care for her, that way she could stay in their home."

"It's nice that you were able to do that for her. Will you be staying in the house or moving back to St. Louis?"

Ruth smiled, "I'm not sure. A lien was placed on their house in order to cover medical expenses so it must be sold."

Karilyne frowned, "I'm sorry... I don't understand. Didn't your mother have Medicare?"

"Of course... but you would be amazed at the amount of things Medicare does not cover."

Karilyne shook her head, "That's really adding insult to injury. So what will you do now?"

"I'm not sure. I no longer have a house or a job, but I pray that God will give me direction... he always does."

Karilyne thought about all of those hours spent at the pond, praying for her mother's healing. Begging

God to give her a few more years. He didn't. And now even more hours praying for the direction that Ruth was so certain would come. It hadn't. She hadn't realized how much anger she still had until now.

"Aren't you angry with God?"

Ruth was puzzled, "For what?"

Karilyne placed her hands on the table and leaned toward Ruth "For losing your job, for losing your home…" the exasperation she had felt for so long was now evident in her voice, *"for not healing your mother…for not answering your prayers!!"*

Ruth swallowed a bite of fruit cake and took a sip of coffee, "I prayed that she be allowed to stay in her home instead of a nursing home and she was. I prayed that I be strong and healthy enough to give her the care she needed and I was. And yes… I prayed that she be healed… and she was."

Karilyne's voice had grown louder "But she is gone…he didn't heal her!"

Ruth leaned forward, placed a hand on Karilyne's and spoke softly "I didn't pray for a specific sort of healing, Karilyne. I didn't place any stipulations on how she was to be healed. I wanted her to be free of pain and I understood that might mean being without her. The moment that my mother entered heaven, she was free of pain... she was healed."

Father O'Brien watched from across the room as the women talked. *Please God, help Karilyne find her direction... her faith.*

The choir had left the chapel and begun wandering through the dining room, the sounds of the First Noel reverberating throughout the church. "Oh! This was one of my mother's favorites... I think I'll join them... how about you?"

Karilyne needed a few minutes alone to process Ruth's last words. "No... thank you, I think I'll just sit for moment."

Ruth stood, "It was really nice talking with you Karilyne.... Merry Christmas and God bless you!"

"Merry Christmas to you too, and please, if you are ever in the village, come to the café… lunch is on the house!"

Karilyne had now become the woman sitting alone at the table in the back of the dining room. Father O'Brien approached with a plate of desserts. "Did you and Ruth have a nice talk Karilyne?"

Karilyne sat back in her chair, her arms folded across her chest. "Let me ask you something Father, how can people who have so little have so much faith?"

Father O'Brien smiled, "And I could ask you Karilyne, how can people who have so much have so little faith?"

Karilyne rolled her eyes, "Gosh Michael that felt like a dig… was that a dig?"

"Let's just say it was a nudge… maybe a poke."

Kurt waved from across the room, holding their coats. "Looks like Kurt is ready to go… it's good to have him back."

Karilyne waved back to Kurt, "Yes... it is. I couldn't have asked for anyone better to care for Grace. I guess I will get to meet his wife and girls tomorrow at Willow Creek... with Jake and the kids gone I plan on being there for Christmas dinner."

Michael's smile faded. "Then I guess you don't know."

Karilyne frowned and shook her head, "Know what?"

"Kurt came back to Allert Village to raise his girls... alone."

Chapter Eleven

"Had to be bikes, Rose?"

Rose giggled, "They needed new bicycles Francis!"

"I know... I know. But next time, have the store assemble them and I'll pick them up!"

"At twenty bucks per bike... no way! Besides, why would I do that when I have a perfectly capable man here?"

The screwdriver slipped and took a small piece out of Frankie's palm. "Son of a..."

"Francis!" Rose scolded in a hushed voice. "It's Christmas eve."

Frankie sighed and sat back on the floor, daubing at the small gash with the tissue Rose handed him. "I'm sorry... I know. Give me a minute and I'll get these finished up."

Rose sat in the chair next to Frankie and placed a hand on his shoulder. "What's wrong? You've been so moody lately."

Frankie knew that he had been and he knew tonight that he had been especially preoccupied since he had seen the woman named Karilyne and a little more than disappointed that he had this chore waiting for him instead of being able to find out more about her.

But there was more to it than that. He hadn't returned any of Angie's calls or, for that matter, any of the other women that he normally hooked up with during the holidays. Something was off. He spent more and more time in the office or the vineyards. More than once he had showered and dressed to do the bar hopping that had been a habit since high school only to find himself in front of a crackling fire, sipping one of his wines and reading the books he was supposed to have read all those years ago.

"I don't know… just the holiday blues I guess. Nothing for you to worry about. You need to concentrate on you and," Frankie pointed to Rose's growing belly, "number four!"

Rose smiled, but the furrowed brow said she wasn't ready to stop worrying, "As long as everything is ok."

"I promise... everything is fine. Now, why don't you go get ready for bed and I'll get these done."

Frankie finished the last bike and placed it with the others under the tree. He put his tools away and flipped the lights off. He walked through the silent ranch style house and found Rose in her robe, sipping tea at the kitchen table, the small room illuminated only by the icicle lights Frankie had strung around the windows.

Frankie sat across the table and helped himself to a reindeer sugar cookie. "All done!"

Rose placed her hand on Frankie's arm. "Thank you Santa... you know how much I... we... appreciate it."

"Don't thank me Rose... it's the least I can do."

Rose stood and placed her cup into the sink. "I'm

off to bed… how 'bout you? Going out?"

"No… I think I'll go back to the barn and get some paper work done."

Rose stopped at the edge of the kitchen, "You'll be here in the morning?"

"Wouldn't miss it! As a matter of fact," Frankie retrieved a box from the back porch, "I have everything we need for Christmas breakfast… hot chocolate, sausages and cinnamon rolls!"

Rose laughed, "Thank God! I was so worried about dinner, I forgot all about breakfast."

Rose padded down the hall and Frankie placed the groceries into the fridge, double checked the lights and locked the back door as he left.

A light snow was falling. He pulled the zipper on a heavy denim jacket, wrapped a scarf around his neck and began the walk to the barn. The gentle hum of the greenhouse generators reminded him that in the midst of all of the cold and snow, things were still growing and spring was just a blink away.

He stopped at the fence that framed the vineyards and thought about the sledding on suicide hill and the snow forts that he and his brother had built in the back yard of the ranch house. Joe was straight A's and Frankie squeaked by with C's. Joe was the debate team, youth and government and track star... Frankie was the quarterback. Joe never missed a day at school or work and he was also the one who covered for Frankie when Frankie had better things to do. Joe loved one girl and Frankie loved them all. Despite their differences they were each other's best friend. The one thing they wholeheartedly agreed on was family. Everyone in the village knew that if you took on one Amante brother... you would have to deal with the other. Frankie dug his hands deep into his pockets and turned to walk the path that wound through the fields to the barn. He could have easily carved straight paths that led from the house to the barn to the fields to the greenhouses but instead he had created beautiful gravel walkways that bloomed with the flowers his mother had loved every spring. He wanted visitors to experience more than just an organic farm... he wanted it to be a wonderland. He hoped to inspire the kids that visited with their parents or those that came on the yearly field trips from the schools to dig deep and watch life grow. He stopped outside the barn door and chose several large logs for the fireplace. Central heating and cooling had been installed when he had decided the barn would serve as not only his office, but his home... he still preferred the sounds and scents that a real fire provided. He slid open the large door to the part of the building that his visitors did not see, flipped on a light and lit the kindling in the stone fireplace. He placed two logs on top and removed his heavy boots. As soon as he was assured of a good flame, he climbed the stairs to the sparsely furnished loft. He slept there only during the spring and fall... those months when opening the north and south doors allowed a cool breeze and peaceful sleeping.

Tonight he slid the heavy steel bar, swung open the north door and looked toward the village. The Christmas lights bathed the entire valley in an electric glow and the steeple at St. James stood tall and majestic against the night sky. *Her name is Karilyne.* He said the name out loud. "Karilyne." He wondered what she was doing… was she still at St. James… was she celebrating the holiday with her family or was it possible she was home alone like him?

He called into the still air, "Where are you tonight, Karilyne?" The birds, startled from their tree top nests, rose in a cacophonous cloud, their wings fluttering against the gently falling snow.

Chapter twelve

Mr. Vandyke whistled to Molly and the sleigh lurched forward, forcing Karilyne and Kurt to hold tightly to the lids that covered their cups of spiced wine. Karilyne wrapped a red and gold checkered quilt around her legs and pulled a fur lined hood snugly around her face. The carolers had filtered out of St. James and split into smaller groups determined to spread Christmas cheer throughout the village. Jaclyn waved as the sleigh passed the Darling family's white Victorian on Main St.

Kurt laughed and waved back. "She's in heaven!"

Karilyne took a sip of the warm wine. "You have no idea!"

The silence in the sleigh was interrupted occasionally by the sights and sounds of the holidays. Karilyne remembered a time when they couldn't stop talking and now they were awkwardly searching for a way to start the conversation.

"Kurt..."

"Karilyne..."

They began simultaneously, then laughed... both nervously sipping.

Karilyne started, "Kurt... I don't want to pry. Michael tells me that you and your girls are here alone... I was just wondering..."

Kurt leaned back against the cold leather seat and closed his eyes for just a moment... gathering his thoughts.

"I'm sorry... it's really none of my business..."

"No... no, please don't apologize. It's just... hard... it's hard to talk about."

Karilyne had thought they were going to talk about separation... maybe even divorce, but she began slowly to realize that when Michael had said "alone" he had met truly alone.

"I met Susan in Africa during my third year with the corp. She was a breath of fresh air. Pretty, red haired, freckled. She was strong and funny and she wanted to help people as much as I did. I fell in love with her almost immediately."

Karilyne smiled and remembered the picture that she'd seen on his desk…the wife and daughters she thought she would be meeting on Christmas day at Willow Creek.

 Kurt shivered and Karilyne unwrapped part of the quilt to cover his lap.

"We worked in some pretty grim conditions, but she never flinched. She was this little ball of energy that never stopped and yet she allowed the others their bad times. When she wasn't helping the villagers she was helping homesick Corp members."

Kurt smiled and shook his head, "She held sick babies in her arms and gave her all to heal them. She celebrated with their mothers when they lived and mourned with their mothers when they didn't."

"After a year of working together we were married by a tribal priest, so the people we had come to know and love could celebrate with us and then again by a missionary priest so there would be no questions!"

Karilyne laughed, "Good idea! I would have loved to have seen the look on your parent's faces when you said married by tribal priest!"

Kurt laughed, "Believe me... my mother still demanded proof!"

The sleigh slowly circled the Allert Village Lake, a brilliant winter moon provided light for the ice skaters and Christmas Eve revelers. Kurt sighed, "We came back to the states when we found out that she was pregnant with Shannon. As much as we loved the people... we wanted our child to be healthy. It was one thing to expose ourselves to some of the dangers, but not fair to ask our new baby to do the same. We moved to a border town in Texas, opened a clinic and life was perfect. When

Shannon was two we had Brigitte... both of them the spitting image of their mother! We didn't have a lot, but we were happy treating people who had even less."

The sleigh turned the corner to circle the boulevard and stopped to listen to Jaclyn's group. They sat quietly listening until the strains of Silent Night faded up Main St.

"Please, Kurt... go on if you can... what happened?"

Kurt leaned forward and clasped his hands between his knees. He breathed deeply, his exhales visible in the cold night air. "Then one beautiful unseasonably cool day in the month of August, we took the girls for a picnic. Did the usual picnic stuff, spread a blanket beneath a tree, ate cold chicken... drank lemonade. We walked around the lagoon and raced back to the blanket. The girls heard an ice cream truck and somewhere between the blanket and the truck, Susan collapsed. Paradise was replaced with pain and pills. She died within a couple of months of her diagnosis." Kurt's shoulders dropped, his hands covered his face, his voice barely audible through his gloves. "I was so busy taking care of others I forgot to take care of her."

Karilyne cringed. She knew that feeling all too well. All of the "what ifs" and "if only I hads".

When Kurt began again, his voice was unsteady, his sorrow becoming as much a part of the sleigh as the polished wood and the leather seats.

"I still can't wrap my head around it. We spent years surrounded by disease and death and came home to be safe and instead…"

A warm tear slipped down Karilyne's cheek and onto her glove. "I am so sorry…"

Kurt's hand covered Karilyne's "I needed to be in a familiar place with familiar faces so when Doc Moore called and told me that the job at Willow Creek was mine if I wanted it, I jumped at the opportunity to bring my girls home."

Karilyne smiled and fought to control the tears, "There really is no better place to raise kids!"

"Being home... close to my parents has been such a blessing. Michael has really helped. And, yes, I admit... I wanted to see you."

The sleigh came to a stop in front of St. James and Kurt lifted Karilyne from the sleigh to the newly shoveled sidewalk. The two walked arm in arm through the parking lot and stopped at Karilyne's car.

"I no longer pretend to know what God's plan is. I was certain that he sent me to Africa to care for the people, but I know that he sent me to meet Susan. I was certain that he sent us to Texas to help the people there and to raise our girls... we had it all planned and now I'm home... without her."

The clock in the village square chimed ten times and Kurt checked his watch. "I hadn't realized it was so late... I still have to play Santa!"

Karilyne nodded. "I should be going too, although I have no one to play Santa for this year."

"I'm sorry Karilyne. I know you are going through a rough patch and I spent the entire evening talking about me."

Karilyne shook her head "It's okay...really...another time."

Kurt opened Karilyne's car door and she slid into the driver's seat. "I'll see you at Willow Creek tomorrow?"

"Absolutely. I promised Grace I would be there for dinner."

"Good... you'll get to meet my girls!"

Karilyne left the parking lot and began slowly driving away from the village lights.

Gods plan... Did God have a plan and, if so, what did it mean for Karilyne and Kurt... and Jake?

Chapter thirteen

Anna's dark hair lay in soft curls down the back of her lavender silk dress, the lights from the deck glittered in the silver hair bow that she held in her palm. The dress' pleated skirt bounced in rhythm as she practiced dancing with an imaginary partner. Patricia watched from a chaise lounge, joyful tears moistening her cheeks.

Anna stopped and sat next to her mother, her small hand wiping a tear from Patricia's chin. "Mom, why are you crying?"

Patricia smiled, "I'm just so happy… and a little sad. Happy to see you looking so grown up and beautiful… also a little sad to see you looking so grown up!"

Anna giggled, "It's because you let me wear lipstick!"

Patricia laughed, "Well, only for tonight! Here, let me help you with your bow."

Peter stood in the doorway watching his wife help their daughter get ready for their first father-daughter dance. The black dress slacks, lavender shirt and new shoes were a far cry from the clothes he wore as a musician and professor, but he would do anything for his little girl even if it meant sore feet. "Next year I say that I buy the shirt and then you match the dress!"

Patricia and Anna looked up at the handsome man in the doorway. "Oh! Peter... you look…" Anna finished her sentence, "Beautiful! You look beautiful daddy!"

Peter flipped the switch on the stereo, lifted the needle and placed it on track four. Sinatra's smooth voice began Moonlight in Vermont. Peter bowed and stretched his hand out to Anna, "Would you care to dance, little one?"

Anna giggled, "I don't know how to dance slow!"

Peter smiled, the deck lights shining in his eyes. "Then I guess I'd better find someone who can

show you" He turned and bowed, "How about you
madam?"

Patricia rose from the chaise lounge and curtsied,
"Why yes kind sir, I would love to!"

Anna watched her parents sway slowly together,
her father's arm around her mother's waist, her
mother's cheek resting on her father's shoulder. The
song ended and Anna watched as Peter cupped
Patricia's chin and gently kissed her.

Anna giggled, "Come on Dad... I don't want to be
late!"

Peter laughed. "We can go as soon as you finish
getting ready."

Anna frowned, "I am ready!"

"Not quite... wait right here."

Peter retrieved the box that held the lavender wrist
corsage he had ordered the day Anna had chosen
her dress. He paused for just a moment and looked
through the cellophane lid, he smiled at the thought
of this, her first corsage and the countless colors in

the years to come until the final bouquet on her wedding day. "Here little one."

Anna slipped the corsage onto her wrist. "It's so beautiful!"

Peter kissed her forehead. "Almost as beautiful as the one wearing it."

Patricia stood at the front door holding their coats. "Ok, you two. Have a good time... drink lots of punch and Oh! Wait a minute... let me get the camera."

Anna shifted impatiently in her new shoes. "Come on mom! We are gonna be the last ones there!"

Patricia ran down the stairs, camera in hand. She snapped several quick pictures of her husband and daughter and then traded places with Peter. She held Anna's hand in the air pointing to the corsage and then knelt next to her, their cheeks touching. Peter opened the door and Patricia took one more look at her beautiful little girl "Have a wonderful time. I will see you when you get home."

"No you won't mom… remember?"

Patricia felt a chill, "You don't come home do you?"

Anna smiled and shook her head, her image fading into the soft evening air, her perfect, tiny hand slipping from Patricia's.

Patricia woke to the silence, her breathing rapid and her hand outstretched. Snow had seeped through the cracks in the bedroom window and the light from the moon glittered against the white just as the lights had glittered on the deck. She ran from her bedroom to the fireplace mantel, grabbed the small urn and collapsed to the floor. She clutched it tightly to her, rocking and sobbing.

A sudden noise on the front porch brought Patricia's head up. Two eyes peered through the windows its breath melting the frost that covered the thick, glass panes. She slipped her snow boots on over her long underwear and grabbed the down filled jacket from the peg just inside the front door. The door's opening forced the doe to bolt. Patricia ran through the snow, her boots leaving deep imprints beside the deer's shallow ones. She ran through the woods, the same bare branches that allowed her glimpses of the deer grabbed at her hair and formed deep scratches on her face.

She couldn't be sure how long she had been running or how far she was from the farm when she reached a clearing. The doe stood in the middle, the moonlight creating a glistening pool in the white snow. They stood motionless... staring at one another for several minutes. "You're looking for your baby aren't you?" The doe called out and waited, the branches on the far side of the clearing snapped and the fawn ran to her mother's side. The doe nuzzled the young deer as though checking for signs of injury and maybe, Patricia thought, promising they would never again be apart.

She began to walk towards the pair her hands out-stretched when they bolted back into the woods. She raised her hands toward the sky, her palms open and dropped to her knees, oblivious to the numbing that had crept into her bones.

"I'm sorry. I'm sorry! I'm sorry!!" Her voice pleading into the falling snow for the forgiveness she could not find within the aching chambers of her heart.

Frankie was startled from a deep sleep, somewhere in the distance he heard what he thought was a woman's cry. He opened the front door to the barn and listened intently but heard nothing save the sound of the wind. He lifted the rifle from its cradled rack and walked into the wintry night, his eyes scanning the farm for any signs of a coyote. He stopped at the fence that bordered the vineyard. A sudden gust of wind lifted the newly fallen snow off the fence into Frankie's face, forcing his left arm up to shield his eyes. The wind stopped as suddenly as it had begun and Frankie lowered his arm. The doe and her fawn were standing just a few feet in front of him... unmoving... unblinking...

their breath mingling with the swirling snow. Frankie smiled and leaned the rifle against the fence, "You got one beautiful baby there." The doe tamped her hoof into the snow and turned towards the bare vines. Frankie laughed, "Help yourself!" He lifted the rifle and turned to walk back to the barn, but stopped to look at the starlit sky. "I miss you Joe... Merry Christmas."

Karilyne was still wrapped in the warmth of the wine and the confusion of the entire evening when she drove over the hill, her headlights catching the flakes of snow that drifted across the country lane. She was reaching for the volume on the radio when, suddenly, the doe and fawn she had seen earlier in the day leapt across the fence and stood in the middle of the road. Karilyne's foot shifted reflexively to the brakes, the car fishtailing and then a slow motion stop just a matter of inches from the deer. Her hand hovered above the horn for only a moment. She slowly pulled the handle on the car door…holding her breath, she lowered her boot gently into the fresh powder, the frozen layer beneath crunching only slightly under her weight. She stood, just inside the open door, reveling in the majesty of the snow, the deer and her fawn. The pair lingered for just a moment before entering the woods. Karilyne tilted her head towards the sky and looked for the northern star, the star she had wished on for countless Christmas'. "I miss you mom… Merry Christmas!"

Chapter fourteen

The parking lot at Willow Creek was full. Family, friends and staff all worked hard to make the holidays special for the residents. Karilyne grabbed the poinsettia and gold foil wrapped box of shortbread cookies that Grace loved so much. She stopped for a moment and took a deep breath. She had spent a mostly sleepless night. The few times she had been able to dose off her dreams had been a jumble of Jake and Kurt, the snow and the deer. She had spoken with Jake for only a couple of minutes… long enough to wish him an insincere Merry Christmas. She told him that she would be spending Christmas with Grace… she didn't mention Kurt.

The lobby's Christmas tree was covered with a variety of ornaments that the residents made during craft classes and the Willow Creek brochures and activity calendars that normally covered the large, round, mahogany table had been replaced with a beautiful nativity complete with the camels that had been carved from olive branches Mrs. Anderson had brought back from her trip to Israel.

Karilyne was met in the hallway by one of Willow Creek's nurses. "You should know that Miss Grace is having a wonderful Christmas… it just isn't… umm… this Christmas."

Karilyne understood. Many times, especially during the holidays, Grace's mind wandered back to those years at the cabin. Karilyne paused just outside Grace's door, closed her eyes and pictured the towering evergreen that stood in the large picture window in the cabin's front room. When she was old enough, her grandfather, Angus, would take her deep into the woods just beyond the edge of their property and cut it down himself... even now Karilyne could almost smell the pine. She felt her eyes begin to tear and she scolded herself. *Not today… today is going to be a happy day. It's Christmas and I am going to meet Kurt's daughters.* She prepared herself for whatever or, whomever, waited in Grace's room, turned the knob and entered.

"Merry Christmas! I come bearing gifts!"

Grace looked up from the collection of Christmas cards that were strewn across her bed, "Merry Christmas! Oh goodie... cookies!"

Karilyne laughed, "Yes, of course cookies, but not too many, I don't want you to spoil your Christmas dinner."

Grace shook her head as she tore the paper from the box, "Don't worry, I won't... you know how much I love turkey. Now, sit down, I want to talk to you for a minute about Karilyne."

Karilyne's heart sank. She began the correction that she knew would be pointless, she wasn't Karilyne today, or at least for this moment, she was instead, her mother, Mary.

Grace opened the box of cookies and offered one to Karilyne.

"Karilyne wants to go away to school and you need to let her."

Karilyne was confused. She *had* gone away to school and even though her mother had suggested the community college in the city, there hadn't been any discussions to dissuade her once she had announced she wanted to go away. Had her mother had this talk with Grace... was it the reason she had acquiesced?

Karilyne thought before she answered. What would mom have said, "Yes... I know, but I would rather that she stays at home and start at Sangamon State. It would be more economical."

Grace shook her head, "It has nothing to do with money and you know it." Grace leaned forward and took Karilyne's hands. "Mary, I know that you are afraid, but it's time to let her go... she will be alright."

Karilyne looked into Grace's blue eyes, "How can I be sure?"

"You can't… that's how life works. We couldn't be sure all those years ago that you would survive… but you did. You weren't sure that you were going to be able to raise Karilyne on your own after Richard died… but you did. Now it's her turn. You need to tell her that she is strong. Tell her that you trust her decisions. Tell her you are proud of her and then… send her on her way."

Karilyne and her mother had never had that conversation. Her mother had quietly helped her pack and dutifully shopped for dorm room necessities. She gave her a credit card and told her to use it responsibly. Karilyne had always thought that her mother questioned her decision to go to a major university because she doubted Karilyne's capabilities… could it be that she had just been afraid of one more loss?

Grace turned to place the box of cookies on her bedside table. She gathered the Christmas cards and stood them single file across the window ledge.

Karilyne wasn't sure if the conversation had ended because Grace felt she had made her point or if she was waiting for further argument from Mary. She waited patiently for several minutes until she knew dinner was soon to be served.

"Mom... are you ready for dinner?"

Grace turned back and beamed, "Karilyne! Finally... I'm starving... smell that turkey?"

Karilyne laughed. Doc Moore had warned her that these sudden changes were just the beginning. Mistaking her for her mother and slipping back to those days in the cabin would eventually change to not recognizing Karilyne at all and for the time being she should be grateful for their weekly conversations. "Yes, I smell it! Let's go get a good seat."

The folding doors that separated the dining room from the activity room had been opened and tables added to accommodate families. Each table draped in white linen and each place set with Christmas dishes and polished silver. The upright piano had been polished and tuned and ready for a holiday sing-a-along.

Kurt had arrived early enough to switch some dining table place cards to be certain that Karilyne and Grace would be sharing a table with him and his girls. Although his mother was cooking a huge meal, the girls had insisted that they spend some time with the residents they had come to know through the times they volunteered while Kurt worked. "Don't worry Grandma, we'll only eat a little and absolutely no dessert!" They had dressed in their new Christmas dresses and convinced Kurt that he should leave the white coat at home for the day and wear a suit and the stethoscope-wearing reindeer tie Santa had left. He was constantly amazed at their resilience. Their capacity to keep giving even after such a great loss… they were just like their mother.

Brigitte seated herself at the piano and began to

play Christmas carols as the residents began to slowly filter into the dining room. Shannon helped those without family to their seats. Father O'Brien was pouring eggnog from a Santa pitcher into small, plastic cups. The scents from the kitchen wafted through the dining room and the chatter grew louder as the tables filled and the excitement built.

Karilyne wheeled Grace through the dining room and helped her into a seat. "Grandma, will you be ok for a minute? I want to peek into the kitchen." Grace waved a frail hand at some residents at a neighboring table and smiled, "Yes... go. No tasting!"

Karilyne laughed. "I won't... promise."

She navigated her way through the maze of tables, accepted a cup of eggnog from Father O'Brien and carefully opened the kitchen 'in door'. Kurt was, what else, carving turkeys.

"Careful Doc... watch those fingers!"

"Hey! You're here!" Kurt waved a carving knife at Karilyne, bits of turkey scattering across the stainless steel table.

"Of course... where else would I be?" Karilyne stood on the opposite side of the table, moved the full platter to the counter and replaced it with an empty one. Kurt heaved an exaggerated sigh, "Slaving away in the kitchen without even a minute to taste."

"You sir, are a liar!"

Kurt feigned shock, "I beg your pardon?"

"I might have believed it if one of your reindeer didn't have gravy on his stethoscope." Karilyne pointed to the spot on his Christmas tie. "Should have worn an apron."

Kurt looked down at the spot. "Oh no!... the girls got me this just for today."

Karilyne dampened the corner of a dish towel. "You keep carving and I'll get the spot."

Karilyne treated the stain for just a little longer than

was necessary. Being close to Kurt... laughing with Kurt was exciting and comforting and familiar.

The counter's serving doors slid open and Arlene poked her head in, "The natives are getting restless, should I cue Father for the blessing?"

Karilyne guiltily dropped the towel and the two of them blushed as Kurt stammered a yes. They loaded the platters and serving bowls onto the serving trolleys and wheeled them into the dining room. Father O'Brien said the blessing and the Scouts delivered a platter of turkey and the trimmings to each table.

Karilyne took her seat next to Grace and Kurt took the seat on Grace's other side. He waved to his daughters to join them.

"Karilyne I would like for you to meet my daughters, Shannon and Brigitte."

The girls smiled. "Hi! It is so nice to meet you. You were dad's girlfriend a long time ago!"

Karilyne eyes grew wide. "Well... yes, I was."

Apparently she had already been the topic of conversation at Kurt's house.

Shannon continued, "He showed us a picture in the yearbook Grandma has at her house."

Brigitte chimed in, "You look just like your picture! Dad had more hair."

Karilyne and Kurt laughed. "Ok… enough, you two, let's have some dinner."

"Not too much, remember dad… we promised Grandma."

The afternoon progressed with gifts for each resident, including a box containing scones and a beautiful jar of strawberry preserves, each label bearing the name of the recipient in meticulous calligraphy.

"Kurt, these are beautiful. Where did you get them?"

Kurt opened a jar, placed a dollop on a scone and handed it to Karilyne. Karilyne took a bite and closed her eyes. "Mmm, this is incredible! They taste like the scones Grace used to make and this jam tastes as wonderful as the jars look."

"They were an anonymous gift for the residents."

"I don't understand... we know everyone in the village."

Kurt shook his head. "Not everyone. We got a call from a woman requesting the names... first name only... of each resident and, last week, several boxes containing these jars were left outside of the front door."

Karilyne raised an eyebrow, "Interesting... a mystery in the village."

After the gifts were desserts and carols led by Kurt's girls.

Karilyne checked her watch. It was late afternoon and there were things that needed to be done at the café before she could go home. "I am going to have to leave, Grandma... are you ready to go back?"

Grace was tired but clearly not ready to leave the festivities.

"She doesn't have to leave yet… we are going to do some more singing. I'll take her back to her room when she is ready… don't worry Mrs. Callahan."

Karilyne's heart swelled with emotion. It was difficult to believe that these young girls could exhibit so much grace. Kurt had said that he wanted the girls to have the gift of a small town and the love of family and friends, but after only a couple of hours it was clear to Karilyne that these incredible girls were the real gift.

"Thank you, Shannon… I appreciate it and I know Grace does."

Kurt stood and placed his napkin on the table, "Girls, I am going to walk Mrs. Callahan to the door. I'll be right back."

One of Willow Creek's nurses approached the table.

"Sorry, Doctor, we have had our first casualty. Mr. Clark has an upset stomach and insists that you see him."

Kurt sighed, "Sorry Karilyne."

"It's alright...really." The truth was that Karilyne was talked out and tired. She was ready to go home, light a fire and open a bottle of wine. There would be plenty of time to talk to Kurt. "I will talk to you soon."

Karilyne bent and kissed Grace's flushed cheek. Grace placed her hand on Karilyne's cheek, "Thank you... it's been a lovely day, but you had better get home to Jake and the kids."

Karilyne felt a pang. *If only that were true.*

Karilyne smiled, replaced the soft pink sweater that had slipped from Grace's shoulders, "Yes Grandma, I'm going."

As she turned to go Grace grabbed her sleeve, her voice in earnest "Karilyne... don't be afraid to smell the roses."

Karilyne looked out the window at the snow covered ground and laughed, "Ok, Grandma... I promise."

Chapter fifteen

January, February, and March passed in stoic Midwestern fashion. Talk of snow and ice and wind chills. Some days were exceptionally busy when a local bed and breakfast would bring a bus of tourists to Karilyne's for lunch and other days the time would have crawled save for Jaclyn's insistence that they begin to experiment with the new soups for the spring and summer.

She spoke to Jake occasionally and, even then, briefly. He insisted that there were still major problems with the project and Karilyne tried to believe him. Josh was still happy in Europe and Jillianne came home aching to go back. She told Karilyne that she had decided she wanted to be a chef and she wanted to study at Le Cordon Bleu… in Paris.

"We will discuss it this summer." Karilyne had said. *I sounded just like my mother. Why hadn't I said spread your wings, Jilly… be happy… you only get one chance to live your life.* She was overwhelmed with the feeling that she had only pretended to live her life. She had done, for the most part, what was expected… what was safe.

She spent some time with Kurt and even with his girls. They came to the café for weekly cooking lessons. She took them to the occasional matinee in the city and shopping for nothing in particular. They reminded her of when her children were young…when they needed her. Bottom line was that Jake, Josh and Jilly no longer needed her….Kurt and his girls did.

She remained steadfast to her morning ritual tramping through snow, climbing over branches, slipping on ice and then, one morning in late March, Mother Nature blew a warm breeze through the village and began, just barely, to transform the landscape from white to green. Karilyne changed her heavy winter coat to a sweatshirt, her snow boots to rain boots and resolved that this spring

there would be answers... change needed to

happen... her life needed meaning... *no matter what.*

Spring

Chapter sixteen

Springtime came to the village it seemed, overnight. One morning Jaclyn awoke to the sound of bird songs outside her window. She yawned, stretched, and smiled. Karilyne had placed Jaclyn in charge of all of the shopping and, although watching their business grow had been rewarding it had also proved to be a difficult task to find as much of the quality ingredients they needed and the late nights and weekends had convinced her that another pair of hands was definitely going to be necessary. So starting today, Jaclyn was on a mission to find both. The café had closed for a few days in mid- March to allow for the installation of a new oven. Jaclyn had taken advantage of the time to check out one of the new cafes in the city. She had ordered soup and salad. The soup had been mediocre and did not compare to any of their creations, but the salad… the salad was a different story. Even in the midst of winter, the greens had been bright and fresh and the tomatoes bursting with deep flavor, far superior to the produce she was purchasing at the local grocers. She asked the waiter for the name of the supplier and learned that his name was Frank and that he owned a large organic produce farm and winery several miles outside of the village. Jaclyn was determined to find him today.

Finding the extra pair of hands, they needed was going to be difficult... it couldn't be just anybody. It had to be someone who fit in with the rhythm that she and Karilyne had created, but she believed that the same forces that had brought her to the village and, more specifically, to Karilyne's Korner, would help her find the perfect person.

She pulled on a pair of cuffed, denim pedal pushers and a second- hand yellow cardigan with a border of white daisies she had embroidered around the hem and wheeled her bicycle from its winter- time resting place in the mudroom on the rear of the house to the back porch. She kicked the kick- stand into position and checked the tires, the basket, and lastly the horn. She tossed her back- pack into the white wicker basket and tightened the red leather straps that secured it to the red and silver chromed Huffy. She tied the plaid ribbons of a straw hat under her chin, pedaled down the drive onto Main Street and headed west.

She rode at a leisurely pace, waving and calling out to the neighbors she remembered as a child and to all of the new families who had become a part of the village's life since she had returned. The warm breeze and budding spring blossoms had everyone in the village outdoors. Mrs. Miller was tending to the rose bushes that lined her cobblestone walkway. Mr. Ryan was taking inventory of gardening tools: rake, hoe, shovel, and spade.

Jaclyn passed the grocers, the café, and the antique store. She slowed at the top of suicide hill and, arms in the air, her fingers reaching toward a blue sky, she coasted, the ribbons from her hat fluttering behind her. At the bottom of the hill, she grabbed the handles and began pedaling furiously surmising that she had approximately six miles to go before she should begin to see signs of the farm.

Frankie's boots were covered with spring dirt and cow manure. Shadows of sweat had begun to appear under his arms and across the back of the blue Henley that pulled tautly across his broad shoulders under his coveralls. It was nine thirty and he had already been at work for hours. He stopped for a moment, retrieved an oversized handkerchief from his back pocket, and wiped the sweat from his brow. He leaned heavily against the shovel and surveyed the fields. Most of the plants that he had nurtured in the greenhouses had now been planted in the soft, warm soil leaving room for the new seedlings...the circle of life...it went beyond being a livelihood, although Frankie would never admit to anyone, the plants, the soil, the sun touched something so deep within him that he had never been able to put it into words. He often wondered if the reason he had distanced himself from women had less to do with the lack of commitment, but rather that he had yet to find a woman he could entrust with his fields, his vines, his soil... his heart. He lifted the shovel, threw it into the back of his truck, and began to walk down the newly formed rows when in the distance he saw someone approaching on a bicycle. He shielded his eyes against the spring sun and watched as a tall, slender girl parked the bike and took a long drink from a bottle of water. She removed a straw sun hat, tossed it into the bike's basket, and peered into his office through a white framed window. She took a seat on one of the wooden Adirondack chairs that sat just underneath the window, apparently determined to wait for, Frankie assumed, him. Jaclyn sat with her long legs stretched out in front of her, content to sit in the shade of the building's awning. The smell of freshly overturned dirt and spring lilacs gave her a sudden rush of joy and she sat with her eyes closed taking deep breaths. The sound of footsteps in gravel brought her to an upright position. The man walking towards her was tall and broad and, Jaclyn supposed, strong. He was using a large, blue kerchief to wipe the dirt from his hands, his work boots creating small clouds of gravel dust as he walked towards her. She stood and the bottle of water that had been resting in her lap dropped to the ground and rolled towards him, its contents forming a small stream. Frankie retrieved the bottle and smiled as he extended his hand to a paralyzed Jaclyn.

"Not much left… come on in and I'll get you a new one."

He walked past Jaclyn and into the small barn that served as the farm's office. Jaclyn stood staring at the door, willing herself to take a step. A moment passed when Frankie appeared in the open doorway, "Are you coming in?"

Jaclyn nodded and walked into the office.

Frankie pulled out a wooden, ladder backed chair and waited for Jaclyn to sit. Jaclyn silently commanded her knees to bend allowing her body to lower onto the seat. Frankie seated himself across the desk from her and smiled again. "What can I do for you?"

"I... I... I" Jaclyn heard herself stammering and prayed that it would stop. She had never seen anyone so beautiful... maybe not even Karilyne. The warmth and wind had shaped his thick black hair into a mass of curls, his deep brown eyes framed by lines formed by suns and smiles. She took a deep breath and a gulp from the bottle that Frankie had handed her. "I want your tomatoes!" There was a moment of silence before Frankie began to laugh... a beautiful, deep laugh. Jaclyn felt herself turning as red as the chrome trim on her bicycle. She wanted to cry, but she reminded herself that she was here for the good of the café. This was important business and Karilyne had entrusted it to her, she wasn't going to let her down. She sat up straight in the chair, folded her hands in her lap and with as much authority as she could muster said, "I am one of the chefs at Karilyne's Korner and we are interested in purchasing your produce." She relaxed, slightly, pleased with the tone in her voice and the fact that she had said chef.

Frankie frowned, "Karilyne's Korner… Karilyne's Korner. Oh! I know that place. It's next to the antique shop on main. I thought she grew her own produce."

Jaclyn was pleasantly surprised that Frankie had heard of the café. "We have been growing when possible, but we do not have the facilities necessary to grow during the winter so I have been buying from Mr. Kent. I recently had the opportunity to sample some of your harvest and found it to be exactly what we need at the café… are you interested?"

Frankie thought for a moment. Karilyne's Korner was the only café in the village. He normally delivered to the larger tearooms, bed and breakfasts, and cafes in the city so it would mean a special trip but he was intrigued. He had heard about the beautiful and mysterious Karilyne even before he had caught a few glimpses of her at the St. James Christmas dinner. He had wondered how he would be able to meet her and now opportunity was knocking in the shape of a slip of a girl with pigtails and skinny legs. He stood and held his hand out to Jaclyn. "Let me give you the five cent tour and we will see if I've got what you want."

Oh my! Jaclyn thought *I have no doubt.*

She stood and accepted his outstretched hand, hoping that he wouldn't notice how damp her palms were. Frankie handed Jaclyn a large wicker basket with a braided handle and walked towards the newly planted rows. She followed, watching as Frankie bent and carefully cut red leaf lettuce, spinach, and butter-crunch. He dropped each fresh morsel into Jaclyn's basket. He continued at a quick pace and Jaclyn made certain to keep up even running into him on a couple of occasions when he stopped without warning. He squatted next to wire baskets, his thighs, no doubt made strong from daily farm work, bulged against the denim as he picked plum, cherry, grape, and beautiful golden tomatoes. Red and green bell peppers, cucumber and carrot, and, finally, oregano and basil.

"There, that should do for a start."

He took the basket from Jaclyn and began the walk back to the office and Jaclyn realized for the first time that they were several miles from the barn. She was, in fact, standing in the middle of fields that seemed to go on forever. She bent to scoop up a handful of earth and sifted it back and forth between her palms, breathing deeply. She opened her arms wide, tilted her head back, eyes closed and allowed the warm kernels of earth to drop to the ground... giggling with pure delight!

Frankie had walked about a mile through the rows when he realized it was only him and the basket. He turned back, shielding his eyes from the sun and frowned. He saw the strange little creature that had followed him dutifully through the fields now standing with her arms outstretched, dirt falling from her open palms and, he could have sworn, laughing.

He started to turn and continue to the office, but something stopped him... he felt compelled to watch her... someone else reveling in something as simple as the feel and smell of new earth. Granted, he had never stood in the middle of a field, laughing and well, playing with the dirt but he understood it.

Jaclyn brushed her hands across her back pockets and began walking through the rows wishing that she could stay on the farm all day. Maybe she could offer her help but she knew she would never have the nerve. Instead, she should just concentrate on the task at hand... securing this produce at a good price. She had fully composed herself by the time that she arrived back at the office and was ready to begin dickering but the sight of Frankie standing at a deep, porcelain sink gently washing the newly cut lettuce and plucked tomatoes took her breath away. He finished with the vegetables and, cupping the cool water into his palms, he splashed it onto his face, his long fingers tracing his cheekbones, chin, and neck. She felt her pulse quickening and the beating of her heart forced her hand to her chest. Frankie smiled and nodded towards a small, round table with two farmhouse chairs that matched the one at the desk, the damp, dark curls swinging with the motion, "I'll make a small salad and send the rest of it back for your Karilyne to sample."

Jaclyn seated herself and looked around the barn. Jars of dried tomatoes, vinegars and oils lined the shelves of a door-less hutch. The multi-colored drawers on two, large apothecary cabinets had neatly placed labels under each brass knob with the name of the herb held within. Photographs of the farm in its fledgling state hung on a knotty pine wall: a small tractor, a pickup truck, a couple of farm hands and Frankie standing under a sparse grape arbor. An oak china cabinet was home to a mixed collection of vintage plates, cups, and saucers. Jaclyn so wanted to open the doors and examine every piece, tracing each delicate pattern with her fingertips. Instead, she remained in her seat tracing the grooves in the worn wood of the table- top.

A warm spring breeze lifted the roughly sewn burlap curtains that framed the small windows on the rear wall of the barn. Jaclyn took a deep breath and wondered if the day could get more perfect when Frankie approached the table with an oversized wooden serving bowl brimming with the freshly picked produce and a crystal cruet glistening with olive oil and fragrant herbs. Frankie smiled as he scooped the salad into the bowl he had placed in front of Jaclyn, "Nothing fancy… I really want you to get the most of what each vegetable should be… the crunch of the lettuce, the coolness of the cucumber, the sweetness of the tomato."

Jaclyn knew exactly what he meant… they were purists. She abhorred the restaurants that covered their salads in thick layers of dressings and cheeses. He was right… the vegetables should speak for themselves. Jaclyn began to reach for the cut-glass cruet when Frankie lifted it and, standing next to her, his left hand resting on the back of her chair, he slowly drizzled a small amount of the vinaigrette he had concocted onto the beautiful mix. Jaclyn watched his forearm drift back and forth… his wrist twisting slightly as he carefully poured the shining liquid infused with sweet basil and pungent oregano. She was acutely aware of the hand that had lightly brushed her hair before settling on the back of her chair and she wanted to lean back, to feel the strong fingers that had so tenderly washed each tomato but instead, she scooted forward in the chair.

Frankie seated himself opposite Jaclyn and filled a second bowl. He waited patiently for Jaclyn to begin, anticipating her reaction to his life's work. Jaclyn sat with her hands folded in her lap.

"Go ahead…" Frankie smiled, thinking Jaclyn was being a little too polite.

"I don't have any silverware."

"Oh! Forks… I'm sorry!" Frankie stood and mindlessly felt the pockets of his overalls. "Um, I don't have any out here… just give me a minute and I'll run to the house."

Jaclyn held her hand up "It's ok." She lifted a large piece of golden tomato with her fingers and took a bite. Her eyelids closed and she chewed slowly, the sweetness of the fruit bursting with each bite. She continued with leaf lettuce and strips of vibrant bell peppers, the oil coating her fingers and sliding down her wrist.

Frankie watched for a moment… puzzled and pleased all at the same time… and then he joined her.

They ate in silence. Frankie watched out of the corner of his eye as Jaclyn reveled in each flavor. She took one last bite and sat back in her chair, wiping the oil from her hands with the white utility rag Frankie had offered as a napkin.

Frankie waited… and waited.

Finally, Jaclyn stood and extended her hand "Yes… I think it will do very nicely."

Frankie stood and accepted her hand, trying not to laugh, "thank you."

They walked back outside to Jaclyn's parked bike and Jaclyn continued with the speech that she had practiced in her bathroom mirror. "I will need for you to stop by the café Tuesday afternoon at 4:00." Frankie sensed that it was important that he simply comply so he nodded, "Yes ma'am."

"Alright then Mr..?"

"Just call me Frankie."

"Alright then, Frankie, see you Tuesday."

Jaclyn pedaled away, willing herself not to look back in case he was still standing there... watching her. *Breathe, Jaclyn, breathe. You did it!!*

Frankie stood with his hands in his overall pockets, pondering the course the day had taken. He would send one of his farm hands on Tuesday's deliveries so that he would be certain to arrive at Karilyne's Korner at 4:00 sharp.

He hoped that the strange girl he had spent the morning with would not only put in some good words concerning his crops but also about him.

He hoped that Karilyne was *everything* he had imagined her to be but more than that, he hoped she was *nothing* like her co-chef.

Chapter seventeen

Jaclyn began the trip back to town, the wicker basket filled with the small garden Frankie had carefully packed in a foam cooler, a mason jar with the herbed olive oil and a bottle of red wine. They had shook hands and Frankie had agreed to stop by the café in two days…that would give Jaclyn enough time to make a presentation to Karilyne and convince her that Frankie's farm was the best choice…the only choice.

She pedaled for a couple of miles and then turned at the sign marked Patchwork Farm. Mr. Andres had been gone for a couple of years, so the vegetables that Jaclyn had become accustomed to swapping for cakes were no longer growing in tidy rows behind the cabin, but spring asparagus and early purple sage continued to grow wild throughout the property. She was so certain they would be growing in abundance that she had already marked the

with her father.

In the small, country kitchen, Patricia was removing the last of six loaves from the oven when the knock came on the screen door. She placed the pan on the butcher-block island and used her foot to close the oven door. She brushed her hands across the butterfly-adorned apron she had found in the kitchen pantry and peered through the wire mesh.

"Hi... I'm Jaclyn and I have a terrible weakness for freshly baked bread."

Patricia smiled. She had spent so many months avoiding any human contact but she knew from the moment that she had created the well in the center of the flour, turned the oven to 350 and dropped the dried sage leaves into the marble mortar that it was time. Time to breathe the new spring air. Time to get ankle deep in new spring dirt and elbow deep in butter and flour. Time to learn how to live with the memories.

The blanket of snow that had covered the cabin for

most of the winter had provided the excuse Patricia

needed for her self-imposed isolation. She spent

most of her time re-reading classic novels, the ones

she had loved so much as a girl... the ones with all

of the happily ever-afters. She played the yellowed

sheet music she found in the bench of the old

upright that had been too heavy to move from its

living room corner. The uneven tones the result of

strings loosened by time and temperature. Patricia

didn't mind... it was how she felt... loose and

uneven.

She had enough food to last the winter delivered

shortly after arriving in order to avoid conversation

or, more to the point, questions. The simple diet she

survived on was a far cry from the dinners she had

prepared in their galley kitchen. Lobsters, crabs,

and clams just outside her front door. Sweet, white

corn and beautiful, ripe berries just outside the

back.   Saturday evenings spent entertaining artists

and musicians, professors and students, fellow

chefs and winemakers. The air infused with sea salt, spices and sweet jazz. Eating, drinking, singing and dancing... always dancing.

"Hello... I'm Patricia... please come in...I could use a guinea pig!"

Patricia dusted the flour off one of the red, vinyl kitchen chairs, offering it to Jaclyn and, for the second time in one day, Jaclyn sat and waited for a stranger to serve her.

The kitchen had not changed except for a fresh coat of paint and new curtains. Mr. Andres had left the table, chairs and appliances. The music came from a small stereo turntable that Jaclyn could see on the living room floor. If there was any other furniture, it wasn't visible from Jaclyn's view point.

Patricia placed a loaf of bread on a wooden cutting board with a crock of butter. She set the table with two pieces of mismatched china and simple tea glasses.

"Excuse me... I've had tea brewing on the back

porch all morning."

"Oh my gosh, the first sun-tea of the season!"

Patricia laughed, "I know! What is it that makes it so much better than any other tea?"

Patricia opened the screen door and stepped out onto the porch. Jaclyn sliced two thick pieces of bread and placed them on the plates. She closed her eyes and inhaled... celery, nutmeg and... Jaclyn's eyes popped open "sage"! *This must be a sign.*

Patricia set the jug of tea on the table. "Very good... yes... sage. I found it growing all over the place."

Jaclyn blushed, "I know. I was here picking the asparagus and sage for tomorrow's lunch at the café when I smelled the bread. I'm sorry, I should have asked."

Patricia seated herself across from Jaclyn and offered her the butter crock. "No, no! It's really ok. I take it you knew Mr. Andres?"

Jaclyn nodded, "Yes. He used to have one of the nicest gardens around and we had a deal...his vegetables in exchange for my pastries!" Jaclyn laughed and continued, "As a matter of fact, I would have to say that I am entirely responsible as to the reason why Mr. Andres was unable to button the sides of his overalls!"

Patricia smiled and Jaclyn noticed a few fine lines framing her eyes. "I never really met him... all of our correspondence was done through letters and the phone, but he sounded like a nice man."

"Yes, he was. I liked him very much... kind of the grandfather I never had."

"I love this place. Why on earth did he leave?"

Jaclyn cocked her head and thought for a moment, "I don't know... I never asked."

A honeybee buzzed through a small hole in the screen door and landed on the bread. Jaclyn leaned forward, her face coming within inches of the bee. "Hello there. I bet you miss Mr. Andres."

Patricia took a sip of tea and gave Jaclyn a sideways glance.

"He had bees… you know… for honey!"

"Really? Interesting. I'll have to see if I could get them started again."

"I can tell you that the café would definitely be a customer. We would love to have fresh honey to serve with the tea and breads."

Patricia tried to sound nonchalant "The café?"

Jaclyn held up a finger as she worked on a mouth full of bread. She swallowed and took a sip of tea. "This is heavenly and, yes, a café. Karilyne's Korner is in the village. Karilyne started it on her own with just a few soups and desserts. I moved back from Chicago and became the pastry chef…"

"You studied at a culinary school in Chicago?"

"Self-taught, really." Jaclyn took another bite of bread, a sip of tea and shrugged. "I had a lot of time on my hands" She rarely spoke about the time she had spent in Chicago and all of the lonely hours she had spent in that tiny apartment. There was no reason to dwell on the past… she was back where she belonged and she was happy.

"I worked in a patisserie after high school and was able to do a lot of experimenting. I use what I learned there at the café. Karilyne leaves the desserts up to me." She was surprised at the amount of pride she heard in her own voice and realized how much Karilyne and the café really meant to her.

Patricia slowly sipped her tea and thought about the possibility of a new life. A reason to get up in the morning. A place where she could share her recipes.

C'mon Patty… now or never. She cleared her throat and began, "I wond…"

"We could use another pair of hands."

The two new friends laughed and continued with their simultaneous train of thought, "That would be wonderful!"

"I don't really have a resume." Patricia felt the excitement that had only seconds earlier lifted her spirits begin to wane as she realized applying for a new job might also mean having to supply information she wasn't ready to give.

"You don't need one."

"Are you sure?!"

Jaclyn laughed, "Positive! Karilyne trusts me. Just stop by the café Tuesday afternoon at 4:00."

Patricia was beaming. "I'll be there!"

Jaclyn leaned back in the chair. This had been quite a day. *Karilyne trusts me...* she hoped this was true. She knew it might take a little convincing but she also knew that Karilyne was very pre-occupied with Jake and that the thought of having some help might just be appealing enough to accept Jaclyn's recommendations.

She glanced at her watch and, as much as she wanted to stay, knew she needed to go. She needed to get Frankie's produce in the cooler, clean the asparagus and dry the sage for the next day's lunch. She stood and Patricia stood with her. "My bike is around front. May I use your bathroom before I start back?"

"Of course… I assume you know where everything is."

Jaclyn walked slowly through the living room, her bare feet leaving prints on the hardwood. A log crackled in the fireplace. A rocking chair placed a few feet from the fireplace was the only furniture in the room except for the piano. A guitar rested in a corner just inside the front door and a wicker basket held cut wood. A painting of the small farm in its heyday that Mrs. Andres had painted still hung in the same place next to the fireplace.

Jaclyn began to turn down the small hallway that led to the bathroom when something on the hearth caught her eye… and then her breath. She recognized them… not because she had seen these in particular, but because she knew what the containers held.

She finished washing her hands and stopped for a

moment to look into the mirror. She whispered a promise to herself and to someone else she was certain was listening "Don't worry... we'll take care of her."

Patricia waited nervously in the kitchen for the questions she was certain would come, but when Jaclyn returned, she simply smiled, opened the screen door, and said. "Thank you for a wonderful afternoon."

Patricia shoulders relaxed and she smiled back. "Thank you! I am so glad you stopped by. I'll walk with you... and here." Patricia handed Jaclyn a loaf of warm bread wrapped in parchment paper. "Oh! And wait..." Patricia opened the curtain that covered the pantry, revealing row after row of jam filled mason jars, "strawberry."

"You made this?"

Patricia wiped her hands across her apron, "I also had a little time on my hands this winter."

Jaclyn nodded. She didn't ask any questions. She

knew that this beautiful stranger had something she was keeping very close. That behind the light brown eyes and the warm smile there was pain. It was true that Jaclyn was young and inexperienced in so many ways of life, but when it came to loss and longing and burying it deep within cups of sugar and bottles of food coloring, she was an expert.

After all, time and time again, her troubles had flown away on countless pairs of marzipan wings.

Chapter eighteen

The dream building that Jake had devoted so much time to planning quickly became a bad dream in the fall and a nightmare by winter. Numerous changes were necessary to accommodate zoning discrepancies and labor disputes created delays. By mid-April it seemed that things were finally on course and, after tying up a few loose ends, Jake would be able to return home. That realization forced Jake to recall that he had left more than just a few loose ends in alert village.

It was Saturday night. Ordinarily, Jake and Karilyne would be having dinner at their favorite restaurant. Instead, Jake ordered room service; a steak dinner and a bottle of wine, changed into a pair of sweats and removed Karilyne's scrapbook and photo album from their protective bag and placed them on the bed. He didn't open them at first. He sat back in the hotel chair, cradling his head with interlocked fingers, closed his eyes and pictured Karilyne on the first day he had met her. Even from across the room, he could see the flecks of gold in her hazel eyes. She was beautiful. She shined. Particularly when compared to the rest of the group that had gathered for the reading who were solemn and intense. The poet, dressed in black, took himself very seriously and clearly did not appreciate the giggling that escalated into laughter from the two people seated on opposite sides of the room. His self-importance probably led him to preclude that a rival poet had placed them in the room to derail his performance. Regardless, within twenty minutes of his debut, Karilyne and Jake found themselves face to face on the sidewalk just outside of the café.

"That was brutal!"

"Please tell me that he is not an English major!"

Jake lowered his voice and quoted a line, mimicking the poet.

Karilyne's laugh brought glares from the group

seated closest to the café windows. Jake took her arm and the two of them ran, laughing, through the snow.

The room service knock at the door brought Jake back to reality. He opened the wine and left his dinner covered. As he began to sip, he opened the first album, the one Karilyne had been keeping since she was a child.

Jake's nature was to hurry, turn the pages and glean as much information as he could in as little time as possible, but not now… he reminded himself that this was too important to rush. He had told Karilyne that the project his company had sent him to oversee would take several months. He knew that she questioned the trip. He truly believed the separation would do them good. Things had become so tense at home that he feared the things that might be said more than he feared being away from her for a few months.

So many things seemed to be up in the air and, to

Jake, it seemed to happen suddenly. Could it be that if had been coming all along and he had just been too busy, too self-absorbed to see it? Probably. He questioned some decisions that he had made. Had he been wrong to work for an established corporation instead of opening his own small firm? It had been so long since he had actually used his own hands to build anything that he had designed that he wasn't even certain, now, that he could. He knew that she missed that... the time that he spent in his workshop creating things for their home. Flower boxes. Deck chairs. Her china cabinet. It was, after all, the artist in him that had drawn her to him. His creativity. His ability to make a simple drawing come to life. She had always said that she loved his eyes, his smile and... his hands. The strong, gentle hands that could coax a piece of wood into a thing of beauty and coax her into bed. Jake sighed and flipped to the first page. The first photos were of Grace standing in front of the

Scottish home that had housed her family for generations. Grace with sheep. Grace, laughing in fields of heather. Grace hiding behind the tall pine trees her family owned acres of. The album progressed with pictures of Grace holding Karilyne's mother and then Karilyne.

Karilyne's school pictures and report cards. Piano recital certificates.

Bits and pieces of fabrics and ribbons. Pressed flowers. Karilyne's memories. Sentimentality and romanticism that Jake had forgotten Karilyne possessed…. the girl in Karilyne.

The second album was their wedding album. The first pictures of them as a young couple in college and in love standing in the gazebo they had visited so often even after they had married. The gazebo where they had spent that first snowy night laughing and talking and, at Karilyne's insistence, where they had been married in the fall.

"It will be cold, Karilyne", her mother had stated.

"Not too cold, mom."

"It could rain."

"It won't."

And it didn't. Mother Nature and Karilyne conspired to deliver the most glorious day of the season. The trees framing the gazebo resplendent in gold, umber and brilliant reds. Baskets of fall mums, red, yellow and purple, and freshly picked apples lined the sides of the concrete stairs that led to the makeshift altar. The guests' chairs had been draped in white with satin ribbons that matched the colors of the fall, gathering the backs into graceful swags.

And then there was Karilyne, glowing in white. Her auburn hair shining through the thin veil and circling her small shoulders. She carried a bouquet of white roses held together with smaller versions of the satin ribbons that adorned the chairs. She was beautiful.

It had been a perfect day… one of the best days of

his life, but there had been other magical days in their marriage. Their first house, the one they had designed together. The days that Josh and then Jilly had been born.

Jake reached for the third and final album. His favorite one. He held it tightly to his chest for a moment, closed his eyes and whispered a plea for help, a prayer for guidance. Maybe somewhere in this book lay the answers. Maybe hidden within the smiles, the bright eyes, the tiny footprints, and locks of hair, he would find the answer, the magic....Karilyne's joy.

He laid the book on the leather ottoman and looked out of the penthouse windows. The lights from the city shined brightly through an unusually clear evening. Even months of being there had not endeared Jake to big city life. His firm was most certainly opening a branch in the heart of the downtown district and they had made a hard to resist offer to Jake. Essentially anything he wanted;

the money, the house, the car, if he would agree to manage it. The truth was that he missed the solitude of his house in the country, the peace that he found in the village… he missed Karilyne. At least he missed what they had been.

He took a few bites of steak and another sip of wine, made himself comfortable on the hotel sofa and opened the final book.

Karilyne, radiantly pregnant with Josh and then Jillianne. Pictures of the children as toddlers, adolescents, and teenagers. Birthday parties, Christmas mornings, school plays, and the picnics at the gazebo. Summer days at the beach and snowy day snowmen. Tiny footprints and locks of hair. The four of them at high school graduations… pictures of a perfect family.

Jake closed the book, sighed, and leaned back against an overstuffed pillow, closing his eyes. He would be returning home on Monday and he had hoped it would be with the promise of a fresh start, but he knew from the few times that he had spoken to Karilyne that it was not going to be quite that easy.

I guess it was silly to think that I could find the answers to our future by looking through our past after all, we are not the same people who married, had children... lost people we loved. Come on Grace...help me out here!

As he snapped shut the final book, a piece of paper slid from the back and floated silently to the floor. Jake sat upright and carefully unfolded the paper, smoothing the creases. He caught his breath and his heart.

How could he have forgotten? How could he have thought that the money and success would ever mean more to Karilyne than their dreams?

He found his phone on the foyer table and dialed.

Karilyne was feeling particularly sorry for herself as she spent another Saturday night alone. She sat on the back deck sipping Shiraz, surrounded by the candles she had lit at dusk that now flickered in the night air. Her phone rang and Jakes name blazed in neon on the side table. She hesitated for a moment, her fingers hovering above the flashing phone. She took a deep breath and answered.

Chapter nineteen

"Good morning!" Jaclyn's voice rang out from the kitchen when she heard the front door bell ring. She emerged in an apron splattered with what appeared to be green paint and tomato sauce, a paint brush in her left hand and a wooden spoon in her right. "How was your walk?" sounding maybe just a little too cheerful.

Jaclyn knew that there was more to Karilyne's morning than just a "walk". She was aware of the time that Karilyne spent talking into thin air, hands often times reaching. She was also all too aware of the talk around town. People thought Karilyne might be "losing it" and now that Jake was out of town on his mystery project, they surmised that he had had enough.

"Good, thanks." Karilyne tilted her head and looked closely at the stained apron. "What are you doing?"

"Painting dining room chairs and making minestrone."

Of course. "Simultaneously?"

Jaclyn stood with her left hand and the paint brush on her hip, her right hand and the minestrone spoon, pushing small, wire frames back onto the bridge of her perfect button nose. Her thick blonde hair was tied back with the strings she had cut from a vintage apron. Overly long legs gave Jaclyn the appearance of a gangly teenager rather than a young woman of twenty four.

Her small shoulders shrugged, "How else?"

Karilyne smiled. She had learned some time ago to stop trying to change Jaclyn. Her methods were odd, but she always managed to get things done. Truth be told, she enjoyed having her around since Jillianne had left for school. She and her daughter spoke weekly and, Karilyne thought, had a much better relationship than she had had with her mother, but she had yet to tell her why she truly thought Jake was gone. There was no reason to worry her. Josh continued his studies overseas, concentrating on European architecture and so they spoke less. She was certain that he was probably in contact with Jake more than with her and she was ok with that, after all, they were two peas in a pod. She didn't worry about Josh, he was a younger version of Jake with every bit as much integrity... at least she hoped Jake hadn't lost his.

She smiled at Jaclyn "Just try to remember which hand is holding the brush and which one is holding the spoon."

Jaclyn returned to the kitchen and glanced at the clock. 11:15... she had a few hours to finish the chairs, handle the lunch crowd, bake the cakes and, oh yes... convince Karilyne they needed Patricia and Frankie before they arrived.

Karilyne gathered the handful of mail that had been left on the front counter. She only half way read making mental notes of anything really important and then tossed all of it into the basket under the counter.

She hung her sweater on the first peg in a row of ten and followed Jaclyn back to the kitchen, her fingertips mindlessly tracing the backs of the chairs.

"Lunch crowd should be small today. United Methodist and First Christian are taking a bus of ladies for shopping and lunch at Tara's Tearoom in the city. If you handle the dining room, I'll finish up the chairs and get an early start on the cakes."

"What?" Karilyne retrieved the spoon from Jaclyn's apron pocket and stirred the minestrone.

Jaclyn sighed and spoke slowly, "If you handle the dining room, I'll finish up…"

"Yes, I'm sorry… that's fine."

Jaclyn took a deep breath, now's your chance "You know we need help, right?"

"What do you mean?"

"Help. You and me… we need help." Jaclyn had rehearsed this conversation in her bedroom mirror knowing that Karilyne would be resistant.

Karilyne continued stirring as she added garlic to the pot. "Oh, I don't know. We've managed pretty well so far."

Jaclyn took a deep breath. "Karilyne, remember last Christmas? And that was before we did any advertising. I already have people calling to order cakes! Not to mention the hours we will need to put in here this summer. The planning, the cleaning, the baking, the cooking and the gardening, which by the way is no longer big enough to grow all of the herbs and vegetables we need. You may find this hard to believe, but occasionally I would like to have a day off!"

"To do what? You don't date." Karilyne was sorry the moment she said it. She knew Jaclyn was painfully shy and found it difficult to even talk to a man. She turned from the stove to find Jaclyn, paint brush still in hand, lower lip trembling.

"I'm sorry... I shouldn't have said that. Just because

I don't have a life doesn't mean you shouldn't."

You have a life you have just chosen to ignore it, Jaclyn thought. "It's okay."

"You're right. Although it seems I am going to have plenty of time on my hands with Jake and the kids gone." Karilyne cleared her throat, trying to sound as nonchalant as possible "Jake called last night... he won't be back till sometime this summer."

Oh no! Jaclyn thought *She thought he would be back this week.*

Jaclyn knew better than to offer advice. She was younger than Karilyne and had no experience with marriage or children, but Karilyne had become her family. She loved her and she loved the café and she didn't want to lose either. She wanted to scream *Karilyne, wake up! He loves you... just let him.* But she knew Karilyne would tell her she couldn't possibly understand and maybe she would be right

"I'm sorry Karilyne. I know it's hard but there are a few things you should be concentrating on."

"Like?"

The front door bell rang signifying the arrival of the day's first customers. Any conversation about needing help or more specifically Frankie and Patricia would have to wait.

The lunch crowd was as sparse as Jaclyn had predicted and by 2:00 she heard Karilyne thanking the last diners of the day. Nerves had added to the already enormous amount of energy that Jaclyn possessed so by 3:00 she had painted four dining room chairs and had a dozen cakes lined up for the oven.

At 3:15, she peeked into the dining room and saw Karilyne seated at a table meticulously checking off a list of ingredients received and adding those which were needed.

It's now or never.

"So, as I was saying. There are some things we need to start considering..."

Karilyne looked up from her bookwork. "And as I

was saying... like what?"

"Like more bookwork, more ordering, more baking, we're going to need better produce for some of the salads we're planning and lots of it!"

Karilyne sighed. "Maybe you're right... I'll start looking...."

Oh my Gosh! Jaclyn had her. This had been much easier than she thought.

"No need, wait right here... don't move."

Karilyne sat in one of the newly painted dining room chairs and waited for... what. She called to the kitchen, "What am I waiting for?"

"Just one minute!" Jaclyn retrieved the salad made solely with the produce she had brought from Frankie's farm, his vinaigrette and a glass of water with lemon. She carried them into the dining room and placed them in front of Karilyne.

Karilyne looked at the salad and then at Jaclyn.

"Did you want me to try the salad Jaclyn?"

"Yes, please."

"For any particular reason?"

"Because this isn't just any salad."

Karilyne lifted the cruet, narrowed her eyes and looked into the oil and herbs. "Is this a magic salad?"

Jaclyn took the cruet from Karilyne, drizzled its contents over the beautiful green mix and, using a set of tongs, gently tossed. She unrolled a set of silverware and handed Karilyne a fork.

"Taste."

Karilyne dutifully stabbed a mix of leaf lettuce, tomato and bell pepper.

Her eyes grew big as she took bite after bite after bite, "This *is* a magic salad... where on earth did you get this stuff?"

Jaclyn practically danced to the kitchen to get her backpack. After a full minute of emptying the entire contents onto the table, she produced a yellow sticky note with two names followed by their professions.

PATRICIA: BAKER

FRANKIE: ORGANIC FARMER

"Here... I found them."

"Found whom?"

"The new members of our team!"

"I think I should probably run an ad first and talk to several..."

Jaclyn shook her head. "I don't want anybody else. I like these two." She pointed to Karilyne's fork, "That is his salad, including the dressing made with the herbs he grows." She tore a piece of the bread that Patricia had sent along with a large smear of the strawberry jam and, practically forcing it into Karilyne's gaping mouth said simply, "Her bread and jam."

Right on cue, the bell over the front door rang out as Patricia walked into the café and an eager Frankie entered through the kitchen.

Jaclyn stood in the center of the room, hands on hips... victorious.

A stunned Karilyne swallowed and looked back and forth between the two strangers.

Her first instinct was to say she was very sorry, but a mistake had been made and she wasn't really looking for any help at this time… but she stopped herself, and instead, she threw her head back and laughed, for the first time in a very long time and said, "Welcome to Karilyne's Korner… we are very glad to have you."

And so it came to be that Patricia, a talented baker with a big smile, a bigger heart, an annoyingly cheerful disposition, and a secret and Frankie, an organic farmer with a winery and the body of one of the Roman gods from which his family had descended came to be a part of the daily life at Karilyne's Korner.

Chapter twenty

Day dreaming had never been a big part of
Karilyne's life. It was a waste of time. She was a do-
er, not a dreamer. When she did "dream" for
something, like the café, she made it a reality. She
spent her time getting things accomplished, well,
most of the time. She knew that her time spent at
the pond, those hours of searching for answers that
lay beyond her world of garlic and chocolate could
be considered wasted and then again, maybe not.
She had pleaded to the mist for help, for an answer,
for guidance... and maybe, without knowing it, for
Kurt.

The sun filtered through the gingham curtains,
across the counter and warmed Karilyne's hands.
She watched tiny flecks of bright particles float and
land on her fingertips. She closed her eyes and
thought about Kurt. Her father had nicknamed him
"the whistler" due to the fact that Kurt's nerves,

when walking up the long drive to her family's home, forced his hands deep into the pockets of his Levis while whistling a low, indescribable tune. She could see him now, shoulder length blonde hair, strong, long nose, and chipped front tooth.

Karilyne felt herself smiling when suddenly a pair of hands covered her closed eyes and a low masculine voice whispered in her ear "Guess who?" snapping her back to reality. Her nose told her what her eyes could not…. earth and sweat… Frankie.

"Frankie! How many times have I asked you not to touch me?" Karilyne stood abruptly, indignant… overly indignant, and she knew it.

Frankie flashed a smile that generally made women's knees weaken.

"Come on Karilyne, you know you want me."

"I want your cabbage, not your body."

Frankie's advances had begun the moment he had learned of Jake's extended business trip. Karilyne had not offered any explanations or details… it was none of his business and, besides, she wasn't certain herself what the details were. Often times, now, when the two of them were unloading produce from the back of the truck, he would hand Karilyne a tray, toss a couple easily onto his broad shoulders and, as they walked through the back door of the café, Karilyne could feel his hand placed firmly in the small of her back guiding her to the kitchen. Try as she might, when her hands were filled with the weight of lettuce, carrots, peppers and herbs, she could not get away from his touch and, lately, had stopped trying.

Now she felt the heat rising in her cheeks and tried desperately to dismiss it as indignation rather than, well, anything else.

"Come on. Let's get the trays. I got good stuff for you today."

"That's great Frankie. My back is bothering me today so if you don't mind, I am going to let you unload while I take a look at the inventory sheets."

It is all so confusing... Jake is gone... Kurt is here and being alone with Frankie has become, well... difficult. She would have to admit that there had now been several occasions when sitting on her back deck in the evening air with a glass of wine she had thought about what it might be like to be *really* alone with Frankie. She fantasized about driving out to the farm, finding Frankie in the fields and feeling his strong hands undress her right there in between the rows of sweet basil. She had no doubt that Frankie knew how to please a woman. She had no doubt that he would make her feel very special... for a few hours.

Karilyne picked up the papers that Frankie had carelessly thrown onto the counter and sat in her mother's rocker.

Frankie cocked his head and smiled. "In that case it sounds like one of my famous back rubs should come first!"

Karilyne moaned, "You are soooo predictable."

Frankie laughed. "Suit yourself!" As he walked out the back door, Karilyne found herself frantically fanning herself with the days produce sheets. Jaclyn watched from the kitchen door, holding her breath and wishing that it had been her neck that Frankie's breath had warmed. Guilty for the voyeurence but unable to look away. Their conversation had been inaudible, but she knew it was the same as always. Frankie's slow, not so subtle seduction and Karilyne's feigned indignation.

As Frankie strode through the kitchen, Jaclyn dropped the tray of cookies she had been mindlessly holding. "Dammit!" She knelt to pick up the remains and found Frankie kneeling next to her. "Hey... no big deal! I've always said you could eat off of Karilyne's floors and now I get the chance to prove it!" He smiled and shoved a handful of cookie bits into his mouth. They stood together and Frankie handed Jaclyn the tray. Jaclyn quickly placed it into a large, double sink, shoved her glasses back onto the bridge of her nose and began stirring broth and cream. Frankie leaned over her shoulder to look into the pot. "Hmmm, smells good in here kid" and as he walked out the door, he called over his shoulder "always does!"

Jaclyn stood clutching the wooden spoon, breathing rapidly, tears stinging her eyes. He wanted Karilyne, of course, not her. He thought she was a child and it didn't help that Karilyne was beautiful, sad, and mysterious. Jaclyn was plain, dull, and completely unable to utter a single word in his presence. She sighed and looked down at the torn jeans with the rolled cuffs and the stained apron that comprised her uniform. It's really all she owned…jeans, t-shirts, aprons and a single black dress for funerals. Her hair forever in a ponytail. No makeup… she wouldn't have a clue how to begin. Her mother had been busy putting food on the table and teaching Jaclyn how to be independent and responsible, there hadn't been any time for hair and makeup. Not that she thought a change in wardrobe and a lipstick would really help. She was what she was... and it wasn't much.

She had inherited a decent amount of cash and the little yellow house where she now spent her evenings doing exactly what she did at work, baking and, recently, painting the birds and butterflies that darted in and out of the wildflowers in the back yard and nearby fields. Her father's dying wish was that she find someone special to share the house...and her life. A nice guy that would love her and raise a family "you have so much to offer, " he had said, he just hadn't told her what that was and, as hard as she looked, she couldn't find anything particularly special behind the wire frames or the rolled up jeans.

Jaclyn jumped, startled, as Frankie came through the back door carrying crates of produce.

"Whoa! Sorry kid... didn't mean to scare you. What

could you be thinking about there, all lost in thought?" He smiled that beautiful white smile and lifted the crates onto the large butcher block table. He retrieved a red bell pepper and held it out to Jaclyn. "Here, kid, smell this... like sunshine." Jaclyn stood paralyzed, her hands at her side. Frankie lifted her left hand by the wrist and placed the pepper in her palm. She lifted it slowly to her nose, closed her eyes and inhaled. He was right, it smelled like sunshine, like the soft warm earth that she had sifted through her fingers and... like him. A tear ran down Jaclyn's cheek and splashed onto the pepper. Frankie stopped, the smile now a frown. "Sorry kid...I" Jaclyn closed her eyes and through gritted teeth said "My name is not kid, it's Jaclyn." There was silence in the kitchen.

For the first time in a long time, Frankie felt remorse. He hadn't meant to, but somehow he had managed through his cavalier stupidity to make this tiny, shy girl feel insignificant. He placed two fingers gently under Jaclyn's chin and lifted,

bringing her eyes level with his "I'm sorry…

Jaclyn." Jaclyn burst into tears, ran through the

dining room, past a surprised Karilyne and out the

front door.

Frankie stood in the kitchen doorway and watched

as the front door slammed behind Jaclyn.

"What the hell did you do to her?!" Karilyne

demanded.

Frankie stood holding the pepper Jaclyn had

dropped, "I…."Frankie stammered, "I called her

Jaclyn."

Chapter twenty one

Mary Catherine sat on Frankie's lap, her fingertips resting on his flexed biceps. She leaned forward, her eyelashes fluttered against his flushed cheeks as she whispered "Again," her breath warming his strong neck.

Frankie smiled and gathered the long, dark hair that had fallen onto his t-shirt into one hand while cupping her chin with the other.

"You want to do it again?"

Mary giggled and nodded "Yes."

"I don't know if I have the strength" Frankie teased.

"Pleeez..."

"Ok, but this has to be the last time."

Frankie's strong hands circled her waist, "One, two," and as his voice reached a crescendo on "three!" he threw the squealing three year old into the air, catching and tossing again and again.

She came to rest on his chest and he wrapped his

arms around her, the two of them breathing in rhythm. They sat this way for a couple of minutes, eyes closed, her cheek on his chest, his chin on her head.

Their moment was interrupted by the sound of a baseball hitting the back of the three bedroom ranch house that sat at the edge of the vineyard. "I think it's time to get your brothers for ice cream!"

"Yea!" squealed Mary, "ice cream...ice cream!"

Frankie slid the patio doors open and called for the boys "Joey, Vinny... who wants to go to town for ice cream?"

The boys dropped their gloves and raced for the door, whooping, hollering and elbowing each other. "Whoa boys, slow down!" Frankie laughed as the seven and nine year old launched themselves into his waiting arms. "Where's your mom?"

"I'm here!" the voice came from a very pregnant woman sitting in a nylon-woven patio chair, her feet propped upon an overturned vegetable crate.

"Come on Rose, we're going for ice cream... we'll get you your favorite, a gallon of anything!"

Rose slid a pair of oversized sunglasses down her nose and smiled. "Very funny... and also very true, but I can't."

Frankie's smile quickly became a frown as he hurried towards Rose. "Don't tell me that kid has decided to come today..."

Rose shook her head, "No, no, no. No baby, at least not right this minute."

"Ok, then what?"

"I can't get out of this chair."

Frankie smiled, shrugged and began to walk away calling over his shoulder, "Well then I guess we'll just have to leave you!"

"Francis Vincent... get over here and help me up!"

Frankie laughed and offered his hands, "Ok... on three. One. Two. Up!!"

Rose grunted as Frankie lifted her from the chair. "Yea...ice cream!"

Frankie shook his head, "I'm not sure who's more excited... you or the kids."

"Me... it's definitely me."

A car horn sounded from the front drive, "We'd better go before they decide to drive themselves."

Pate. Cheeses. Chocolate covered strawberries. *No, scratch the strawberries... too romantic.* Grapes and melon. Jaclyn's fresh baked baguettes and raspberry tea.

Karilyne made a mental checklist of the items she had packed for her picnic with Kurt as she sat at the pond. Daylilies bloomed in glorious orange as the ducks swam in and out of them, a game of hide and go seek with their chicks.

She sat back and closed her eyes as the sun warmed her cheeks.

Well, mom. Jake is gone and Kurt is here. Got any thoughts on that? Seems a little too easy, doesn't it? I always swore that if anything ever happened between me and Jake there would be no other man. I'm not saying

that the other man would be Kurt. I guess I was just very

surprised at what I felt when I saw him. I can only

imagine what you would be saying to me right now. Let's

see... you would be telling to get on a plane, go find my

husband and work things out, right? After all, that's

what you would do.

Karilyne stretched her legs out in front of her and raised her fingers to the sky, opening and closing, generating energy. She dropped her arms to the bench and sighed.

"Karilyne. Will Kurt be joining us for the holidays?" Karilyne sat, curled into a round, wicker chair she had purchased with her own money when she had been able, for the first time, to decorate her own room. The book she had been reading lay open in her lap. "No, mom, not this year."

Karilyne's mother seated herself on Karilyne's bed. "What's going on Karilyne?"

"Nothing, mom. We just aren't seeing each other anymore."

She said nothing for a moment, measuring her words before they were poured. "Well, that's too bad. Kurt is a nice boy with a promising future, but, of course, I wasn't dating him." She stood to leave the tiny room bordered by bookshelves and record albums. She turned one last time before closing the door. "Who called it off?"

"I did".

"Ahh."

Her mother's disappointment was palpable. Karilyne's heart had sunk, once more she had been a disappointment, maybe she should call Kurt, tell him she had been wrong. It had been a mistake. What if her mother was right?

She had gone on to college and it was there that she had truly learned to spread her wings. The constant uncertainty diminished as her writing was met with accolades and encouragement from her professors.

She began to perform with a small ensemble in clubs near the campus and it was in one of those clubs that she had met Jake. She had taken him home to meet her mother and it was then that the weekly phone calls that always included an inquiry as to whether or not she had heard from Kurt ended. Jake's beautiful smile, good looks and easy nature won her over. Karilyne knew, also, that her mother was relieved that he wasn't a musician. The very word 'architect' had caused a noticeable relaxing in her mother's posture. Karilyne felt that she had finally got it right. She was graduating, she was in love and, with Jake… had atoned for her breakup with Kurt.

Kurt's name had never been mentioned again… until now.

Her watch sounded the alarm and Karilyne began the walk back to the café.

Kurt waited nervously in his office for Karilyne's arrival. She had agreed to have lunch with him after her visit with Grace and he was as anxious as he had been all those years ago on their first date. He had been in love with Karilyne and he had been inconsolable when he received her last letter. She had insisted that they see other people but, although he asked all of their mutual friends, no one knew of anyone that Karilyne was seeing which simply brought him to the conclusion that it was just him that she no longer wanted to see. There was no other person for him and he was certain there never would be... until he met Susan.

He wasn't sure what he had expected when he came back. He made a list of all the reasons that it made sense;

Close to my parents

A job that will offer security and more time with the girls

Small town life

Fresh air

Good schools

What wasn't on the list was Karilyne.

If he was honest with himself, he would admit that she had always been in the back of his mind when the opportunity to move back presented itself. He knew that she was married, he knew that her children would be grown by now and he learned soon after moving back that her husband was gone on an extended business trip. He was home for months before he had sent word that he wanted Karilyne to meet Grace's new doctor...him.

They had spent some time together during the winter, but never alone outside of Willow Creek or without the company of the girls. In part, to avoid the inevitable small town gossip, but Kurt knew that if they were going to have a relationship beyond friendship Karilyne would have to make some important decisions. She had agreed to a picnic on the grounds of Willow Creek. It would be the first time they were alone, but still safely out of the sight of prying eyes. He was not the kind of man that would break up a marriage, but it was clear that Karilyne's marriage was on shaky grounds and he was determined that, today, he would know with some certainty if there was any chance for a future with Karilyne.

He sat at his desk and looked at the photograph of Susan and the girls. Not enough time had passed that he still didn't expect to see her at any given moment and the ache that he felt was still as paralyzing as the first time that he realized he would never see her again. But what deeply troubled him now was that *just* enough time had passed that when he closed his eyes, he had trouble remembering the sound of her voice. Sometimes in his dreams it was as clear as the bells at St. James. Then, when he would awaken to the reality of the empty place in his bed, he would whisper Susan... Susan... Susan as though saying her name over and over again would keep her in his heart.

Kurt was startled by a knock at the door, glanced at

the clock and knew it would be Karilyne. He took one last look at the picture, a deep breath and opened the door. In a cotton skirt, blouse and coral sweater tied loosely around her shoulders Karilyne looked just like the girl he remembered from high school.

Karilyne held up a wicker basket, "Hungry?"

"Starving... what's in the basket?"

Karilyne smiled, "For starters, pate."

"Goose?"

"Salmon."

"Strawberries?"

"Grapes and melon."

"Scones?"

"Baguettes."

"Iced tea?"

"Yes!!"

Kurt held his hands up, "Nailed it!"

Karilyne giggled, "yeah, you did... scary... almost as though you could see in the basket!"

Kurt laughed, "Here… you cooked… I'll carry."

Karilyne handed him the basket and turned to enter

the hallway. Kurt stopped her and closed the door.

Karilyne was confused, "I thought we were

picnicking."

"We are." Kurt pulled the cord to the curtain

behind his desk revealing a door. He held his finger

to his lips. "Shh… don't tell the inmates."

Karilyne knew that taking the back door meant that

they would be free from the glances of a curious

staff. "It feels like we are cutting class!"

They walked in silence to the small park that lay

just beyond a row of weeping willows. When they

were teenagers, it had been just a clearing with a

couple of picnic tables, but when Willow Creek was

built, it was developed into a park for the residents

and staff. Adirondack chairs placed intermittently

around a shallow fountained pond and new picnic

tables lined the cement floor of a canopied shelter.

Blooming lilac, lavender and honeysuckle

perfumed the warm, spring air.

Karilyne spread a red and white checkered cloth on a sun drenched table and carefully arranged the contents of the basket between their plates.

Kurt took a bite of the pate Karilyne had spread onto a baguette and smiled.

"Good?"

"What... oh, I'm sorry... yes, it's very good. I was just thinking about all of the time we spent here and we were not eating pate!"

Karilyne laughed, "No! Bags of chips and cheap... very cheap wine!"

Kurt sighed and looked slowly over the park's grounds. "We made some big plans."

Karilyne nodded, "Yes... we sure did."

They ate in silence for several minutes, a gentle breeze playfully lifting the corner of the table cloth.

Kurt cleared his throat, "Karilyne... I've wondered all these years... what happened? Was it something I did or said or..."

Karilyne placed her hand on Kurt's, "Absolutely not!" Karilyne closed her eyes and tried to recall those feelings from all of those years ago... that one moment in time when she had decided to write that last letter.

"I just did what I thought was inevitable. You were tall, handsome, smart, and in medical school, I just figured that eventually you would meet someone who was your match."

Kurt gently touched Karilyne's cheek, "I thought you were my match."

Karilyne caught her breath and blushed, taken aback at her heart's response to his touch. "To be honest, I thought that I might have been with you because it was what my mother wanted... not what I wanted. I was young and uncertain and floundering until I went away to college. It was there I found myself..." Karilyne smiled, "and Jake."

Kurt stood and stretched, "Let's walk."

They walked slowly through the park, stopping occasionally at the large containers of flowers that haphazardly dotted the landscape.

"The groundskeeper does an excellent job here!"

"Yes... yes, he does... or she does... or they do..." The two looked at each other and laughed, "Nice small talk! How about the weather or this year's soybean yields."

Kurt frowned, "Word around the donut case at the gas station is they are expecting record yields."

Karilyne giggled, "Thank you... good to know."

Kurt was uncertain of exactly how to continue, in part because he wasn't certain of how much he wanted to know. It would be much easier if Jake simply remained a name... the faceless man who had left her, but he wanted to know... he wanted to know about the man who won Karilyne's heart. He swallowed hard, "Tell me about your husband... tell me about Jake."

Karilyne took a sip of tea, "We met in this little

coffee shop or rather outside of it. We were listening to this really awful poet, everyone in the place was being very serious except for us."

Karilyne smiled remembering the first time she had heard Jake's deep voice. "We were never apart after that evening except for the occasional business trip when Jake had to oversee a project... that is, until now."

"Karilyne you know a lot has happened in your life in a short period of time. Losing your mom... the kids leaving for school. Jake leaving on this business trip. Kind of the perfect emotional storm. I think we get to an age when we start to question our decisions... a time when we realize there are some things we are not going to accomplish... places we won't see and people we'll never meet." Kurt paused, searching for just the right words, "and then we lose people we love and, along with them, little pieces of ourselves."

Karilyne spoke softly, wistfully, "I know... it's hard.

I never worried about what I was going to do because there were always opportunities but that is just not true anymore. I thought I had it all down. I could have shown you a checklist of my perfect life and every box would have had a very neat, solid black check mark in it and now..."

They stopped at the fountain. Karilyne sat on the edge and allowed her fingers to drift through the cool water, the fountain gently splashing tiny droplets of water onto her skirt. Kurt fished through the pockets of his jeans. "Here..." he handed Karilyne a penny, "make a wish."

Kurt paused for a moment and then tossed his coin into the fountain. Karilyne stood and held the shiny penny tightly between her thumb and forefinger. She closed her eyes and imagined a life with Kurt and the girls... someplace where she would be needed, then, just as quickly, she imagined Jake's strong arms around her... his voice soft and low against her cheek as they sat in front of the fireplace in their house… their home. She opened her eyes and let the coin fall into her palm. "I'm sorry… I'm afraid that I have no idea for what it is I would wish right now."

Kurt's heart sank. He came today wanting an answer and had naively convinced himself that he would be okay with whatever that answer might be. He realized now that he had deeply hoped that the feelings they had once had for one another would magically reappear, Karilyne would know that she was meant to be with him and they would live happily ever after as a family.

It was clear that had not happened for Karilyne but even more confusing…it hadn't happened for him either.

Rose, Mary Catherine and Joey sat at the wrought iron table in front of the Summertime Anytime ice cream and treats shop waiting for Frankie and Vinnie to deliver their ice cream orders. This was a rare treat… not just the ice cream, but for Frankie to take time away from the fields or the vines at this time of year was also rare. Rose sighed, placed an oversized shoulder bag behind her and leaned back, basking in a perfect spring sun.

The strong movement in her tummy reminded her that someone else was waiting for ice cream. Although she had several sonograms, she had asked that the sonographer not reveal the sex of this one… they wanted this last one to be a complete surprise!

Karilyne scanned the street for a parking place. She had only slightly nibbled at the picnic she had packed and her mood dictated something sweet… ice cream would be perfect. She stopped just short of the Summertime Anytime ice cream shop and waited for a minivan to pull out of a spot and smiled. A pregnant woman and two little people sat at one of the sidewalk tables obviously waiting for their springtime treats. She thought about all of the times she and her own children had sat at the very same table...*just a moment ago.*

The shop's door opened and a little boy emerged with two cones followed by a man carrying a tray of sundaes.

They sat at the table with the trio and the little girl climbed into her dad's...*wait*...Karilyne's eyes narrowed and she leaned forward in her seat...*Frankie's lap?! Son of a... he's married.*

Karilyne's hands gripped the steering wheel, her heart pounding. The car behind her honked and the driver indicated that she should either park or drive on.

"He's married... with three children and another one on the way!"

Karilyne fumed when she thought of all of his advances *"How dare he! All this time... all of the touches and all of the charm and the entire time he had a beautiful young family waiting for him at home."*

She pulled into her driveway only barely aware of

the time between the ice cream shop and her house.
She sat in the car for several minutes before the
tears began.

Kurt so desperately looking for someone to replace
the wife he claims to have loved so much.

Frankie so easily dismissing his wife and children to
pursue her.

Jake, whose children were grown and all that he
had to come home to was a morose, self- pitying
wife… was he looking for a replacement… was Jake
hoping to find a substitute?

Chapter twenty two

Although she had been awake for hours, the phone's ring startled Karilyne. The clock on her bedside table read 6:00. She fought through the fog of a sleepless night combined with too much wine to temper the anger and confusion, trying to remember what she had scheduled this early on a Saturday morning.

Oh no… Frankie! I agreed to tour the farm and try some of the wines.

She knew, of course, that his plan would consist of more wine than tour and she wasn't entirely certain why she had agreed. She thought for a brief moment about cancelling but instead decided that she wanted to see him. She wanted to confront… to let him know that she knew he was married and that she was disgusted by his actions. She reached for her phone and sent a simple message 'b there by 7'. She didn't want to talk to him until she was ready.

Frankie read the message and smiled. Karilyne was coming. Finally, she would be on his turf. Today, he would have the advantage. She would see all that he had to offer... the farm... his fields, his vines, his life's work.

Weeks of preparation had turned the farm into a dreamland. Each floral and vine covered trellis had been removed from its snug winter greenhouse and carefully snapped into place along the cobbled walkways. Oversized planters that Frankie had picked up at outdoor markets, varying seats, benches and stools, polished, dusted or painted were placed sporadically throughout the farm. He hoped that the headiness of the flowers and the seduction of the wine would help to soften Karilyne.

Wicker produce baskets had been dropped along the path they would follow. Each was to be filled with Karilyne's choices and then collected at the end of the day. Frankie was putting the final touches on a worn, knotty pine table in the vineyard; wine glasses, check... corkscrew, check... ice buckets, check. Watch... 7:00. He took a deep breath, she *should be here.*

Karilyne arrived promptly at seven, dressed in jeans, t-shirt, and tennis shoes. She pulled her hair back into a pony tail, applied sunscreen, lip balm and fished through the trunk for the St. Louis Cardinals visor Jake had bought her at an afternoon game. She stood in front of the barn, hands on her hips... waiting. She looked out over a large expanse of fields. In the distance she could see farmhands busy at varying tasks, but couldn't be certain if any of them were Frankie. She checked her watch at 7:12 and walked to the back of the barn... the sight took her breath away.

Daffodils and tulips grew in an untamed carpet. A crude sign stood at the end of a cobblestone walkway pointing the way to the vineyard and just beyond a wrought iron fence, a fairyland bloomed. Karilyne smiled and decided to start the tour on her own assuming that, eventually, she would run into Frankie. She also thought that the fresh air would help to cure a slight hangover and the walk would give her time to practice her speech.

She pushed gently on the fence's gate, embellished with the animals that frequented the farm; deer, rabbit, and fox and stepped onto a circular stone. Etched into the top of the multi-colored marble read Amante and at the bottom vigneto. In the center, two more words...famiglia and fete.

Trellis after trellis covered with soft blue morning glory, brilliant crimson cypress vine and black eyed Susan vine. Containers of hosta and purple allium, zinnias, and even marigolds placed along the winding walkway. Karilyne stopped at a pergola blanketed with a vine boasting bright scarlet, tubular flowers. It was unfamiliar and breathtaking. Burned into the pergola's front piece the words le vigne di gara. She sat on a small, wooden bench and closed her eyes...the shards of sun that streamed through the pergola's slatted roof warmed her face. She wondered who had created this haven... this beautiful respite. Surely not the man who was cheating on his wife and children.

She felt something against her neck and waved her hand to shoo away the unwanted intruder. "Hello beautiful."

Karilyne jumped. "Geez, Frankie... you scared me!"

Frankie laughed, "Sorry... couldn't resist."

Karilyne ran her fingers through her bangs and tightened the strands already held tautly by a thick band.

"I umm...I waited for you at the barn but..."

Frankie stood with his arms outstretched, a hand on each side of the pergola, grinning that beautiful, exasperating smile.

Karilyne cleared her throat and pointed to the unusual blossoms. "I don't recognize this plant."

Frankie ran his fingertips through the flowers. "Firecracker vine. It opens scarlet, ages to orange, and then finally yellow. I found it in Mexico and had to try my hand at it here."

Karilyne smirked, "Ah! In Mexico... no doubt chasing senoritas."

Frankie frowned. It was obvious that Karilyne had heard about his reputation and assumed that chasing women was his primary life's work.

"Actually I went with a friend to help some of the small villages out with their crops. They needed some alternatives to the way they had been growing so we taught them how to make better use of the resources they had to increase yield and variety."

Karilyne was speechless. It never occurred to her that Frankie was anything more than an overgrown adolescent. She pointed to the words etched into the pergola. "What does this say?"

"Le Vigna de Gara... The Tender Vines."

Karilyne nodded, "It's beautiful... Italian?"

Frankie laughed, "Of course Italian...the Amante brothers' farm and vineyard."

Oh my God... there are more than one of you?! "Will I be meeting the others?" Karilyne was anxious to see what Frankie's brothers might be like.

Frankie had begun to walk back through the floral forest in the direction of the barn and called over his shoulder, "Not others... just one and, no... my brother Joey is deployed in Afghanistan."

Karilyne began to follow. It was becoming clear. Joe was the responsible one serving his country and Frankie was the charming dreamer. She thought again of her purpose in coming today, but decided that, now.... she really wanted to see the rest of the farm before she leveled him with her newfound knowledge and rejection.

Frankie stood at the edge of the perfectly formed rows waiting for Karilyne to catch up. She had been impressed with the vineyard's floral gateway even if she hadn't said so. He figured they would spend the morning picking whatever she chose and then circle back to the table he had ready under one of the heavy laden arbors…. sample some of the wine and then… well… *we'll see.*

Frankie picked up one of the strategically placed baskets. "We'll start with peppers… then cucumbers, eggplants, zucchini, tomatoes. We'll save the herbs and greens for last. Ready?"

Karilyne grabbed the basket from Frankie, "Ready."

Frankie walked quickly through the fields, pointing and picking. He talked about soil quality and planting depths. He explained that the greenhouses and his use of hydroponics gave him an advantage over other organic farmers in the area who still counted solely on the whim of Mother Nature. He told her about the buses of school kids who came every year and the vegetable treasure hunt he sent them on and how much it meant to him to see their faces when they created their own meal from the bounty they held in their baskets.

Karilyne was overwhelmed with the amount of information and completely confused by this stranger who was passionate about growing and giving back… this wasn't the Frankie that she knew at the café… the obnoxious flirt. *The married man with four children!*

After several hours Karilyne began to realize that the daily walk to the village lake wasn't keeping her in the shape she needed for a day on Frankie's farm. The warm spring sun was intermittently replaced by gathering clouds and a cool breeze had begun to rustle through vine after vine when they reached the carefully prepared table.

Karilyne sat heavily into a cushioned wicker chair, leaned back and closed her eyes. The sound of a popping cork forced them open. *Ah! Here we go.* She sat up in her chair and cleared her throat… it was time to let him know that she knew. Knew that he was married. Knew that he had kids. Knew that, although it had been a nice show, it was just a show.

Frankie gently brushed several loose strands of hair off of Karilyne's cheek and smiled. "You look more beautiful now than any time I can remember." Karilyne wiped the sweat from her forehead with the back of her glove, "Of course I do... sweaty, covered with dirt."

Frankie laughed, "Yes! Sweaty and covered with dirt! Here..." Frankie handed her a wine glass and poured from one of the five bottles that lined the table. "Close your eyes."

Ok... one glass of wine can't hurt... it might even help. Karilyne closed her eyes, swirled, sniffed and tasted. "Dry... white... and, um... citrus?"

Frankie laughed, "Yes! Very good...you know wine."

Karilyne opened her eyes and shook her head, "Not really... I like what I like." She took another sip, "I tend to be a Shiraz girl."

"That was a Chardonel. We have a few more whites

to get through before we get to the reds."

Karilyne began to protest when Frankie placed a wooden platter filled with a variety of cheeses, fruits and breads on a mosaic tiled table next to her. Her stomach convinced her to delay the scathing commentary that she had rehearsed while angrily drinking a bottle of Shiraz.

A little bit of cheese and bread can't hurt... it will probably help.

Frankie poured from another bottle. Karilyne swirled and sniffed, "Hmm... floral." She tasted, "Dry... white... light... spicy."

"Yes, a Traminette." Frankie was thrilled. The woman of his dreams was in his vineyard tasting his wines.

Karilyne plucked several grapes from the bunch on the platter while Frankie opened another bottle. "So, how did you get started with all of this?" Frankie sat in the chair on the opposite side of the garden table. "My mom and I used to garden when

I was a kid. Then, it was out of necessity. The garden provided us with vegetables throughout the year." Frankie took a sip of wine. "And then when she died, I continued because it reminded me of her. Eventually I realized that the small garden behind the house wasn't enough so anytime I saved a few dollars I bought another acre and, well.... the rest is history!"

Frankie poured from yet another bottle and ran his fingers through the dark, windblown curls. "I love the yearly challenges of being certain to never allow changes to an heirloom tomato that has thrived for a hundred years and the challenge of altering a different plant to create a hardier variety."

Karilyne took a sip and smiled, "You really love this, don't you?"

"Yes, I... I guess I do."

Frankie opened the last bottle, "Ok... I think you are really going to like this one."

Karilyne began what she knew would be a weak

protest when Frankie poured a beautiful, rich, red into her glass. She followed the routine, swirl...sniff...sip. It was good. It was better than good. She took another sip, "Dry... red... not sure."

Frankie took a sip from his glass, "Cherry."

"Yes... cherry." Karilyne closed her eyes, "Hmm... I like this."

Frankie quietly leaned over Karilyne, "How about this." His lips softly touching her lips.

Karilyne smiled, "Very nice." *Wait... what the hell is happening?*

Karilyne jumped from her chair, knocking Frankie off balance. The sudden clap of thunder masked the sound of the shattering glass against the inlaid stones.

The rain came fast and furious... thunder growing louder and the lightning more intense. Karilyne began to quickly wind her way through the garden pathways in the direction of the barn knowing the parking lot was just beyond.

Frankie followed, "Karilyne! Stop… please."

Karilyne picked up her pace, ducking branches and swerving around the planters. As she reached the gate and lifted the latch, she felt Frankie's hand grasp her wrist. "Karilyne… talk to me."

She turned to face him. His t-shirt was soaked through and clinging to his broad chest. The curls swirled around his head with the bursts of wind. They stood, panting, and Karilyne became aware that her t-shirt had become transparent as well. "I know! Ok?… I know!"

Frankie shook his head, drops of rain hitting Karilyne's cheeks. "I don't understand… you know what?"

Karilyne twisted her wrist free from Frankie's grasp and ran through the parking lot. Frankie caught up with her, placed himself in front of her car door and hollered over the pounding rain and thunder. "Tell me what it is…"

Karilyne just wanted the day to be over. "I know

that you're married. I know that you have a wife and kids."

Frankie shook his head and shrugged... bewildered. "I don't know what you are talking about... I don't have a wife or kids!"

"I saw you at the ice cream parlor with all of them! Please don't make this worse by standing here face to face with me and lying!"

Frankie opened the car door and Karilyne slid into the driver's seat.

She turned the key, and began to roll up the window when Frankie stopped her, "I am not married... that woman you saw me with is my brother's wife and the kids are his kids... I take care of them while he is deployed."

He stood to allow Karilyne to leave, "You saw me with my sister-in-law and my niece and nephews."

Chapter twenty three

It was a Sunday afternoon and Frankie knew that
the café would be closed and yet he found himself
standing on the sidewalk attempting the door
anyway... just in case. Karilyne had left the farm
abruptly after their argument and he was hoping
that her anger at the thought of him being married
meant that she was interested. When the door did
not budge, he shielded his eyes and peered through
the front window café curtains and, although the
dining room was empty, the small beam of light
that stretched across the planked floor told him that
the back door was open. He stepped easily over the
small picket fence that stretched between Karilyne's
Korner and the neighboring antique shop and
walked in between the two buildings towards the
back yard garden. As he began to round the corner
to the café's open door, he heard a voice that made
him stop and back up just to the edge of the

building. He held his breath, and not wanting to be seen, he crouched beside the café... his head leaning against the ivy covered bricks.

She was singing and, as Frankie listened, he recognized it as a hymn... the Garden. "I come to the garden alone, while the dew is still on the roses." Her voice was clear and sweet and her singing stopped only intermittently as she knelt to plant the seeds she carried in various muslin bags tucked tightly into a large basket. Her hair, which Frankie had never seen without the restraints of a rubber band or some sort of tattered apron string, now lay unencumbered down her small back, a gentle breeze lifting each golden strand and then playfully re-arranging them in a crisscross pattern over her shoulders. The glow on her cheeks indicated that she had been working for some time and the smile on her face, as she knelt and dug and sowed, said that this was where she was truly happy.

Frankie inhaled and smelled the cakes baking and then realized *of course she would be here,* even on a Sunday afternoon, preparing some of the pastries for the week ahead. He thought about offering some assistance, but he stopped knowing that the minute she knew he was there she would reach for the rubber band that would tie her hair... and her tongue. Her eyes would stop dancing to the simple songs she sang, her hands would find their way out of the soft dirt and deep into the pockets of her overalls and the back door to the café would swing solidly shut.

So he didn't... instead he lowered himself to the ground, the weight of his broad shoulders sinking into the contours of the bricks, strong hands hanging limply on top of his bent knees, he closed his eyes and listened to the sound of her voice and his own soft breath.

He would stay as long as she did. He would remain silent so that she would not.

The two of them continued in just this way…Jaclyn planting, singing and baking while Frankie sat. Before long, the afternoon light began to disappear beyond the rooftop of the antique shop and the back door of the café closed for what Frankie knew would be the final time that day. He waited for just a moment before walking quickly and quietly to his van hoping to leave before she saw him.

He drove the twelve miles to his farm in silence, fingers tight on the wheel, his jaw clenched… images of Jaclyn and her voice playing over and over in his mind. He had gone to the café hoping to see Karilyne… to see if her husband's absence had begun to wear her down, leaving her vulnerable to the charm that had never before failed him, but now…

Dammit, Francis… come on, get a grip! What the hell are you thinking?

The trouble was he really didn't know. He was feeling something he couldn't quite place. He sat at his desk, staring at the next day's paperwork, the numbers and words jumbled as he tried to make sense of the afternoon.

He closed the books knowing that any more time spent would be time wasted. He uncorked a bottle of wine from the vineyard, poured a glass and decided to check on the crops he would need for Monday. He walked slowly… sipping. His jean jacket warming him despite the steady, cool breeze that ruffled the burgeoning lettuce leaves and his thick dark hair.

What was this feeling of unrest… uncertainty? Why couldn't he get her out of his head? She was nothing like the stiletto heeled, red lipped, mascaraed women that he knew, that he wooed, that he bed and that he left before the insistence of being held implied that there were any true feelings involved. That's how he liked things. Simple, and on his terms.

But he had wanted to hold *her*. He wanted to smell

her hair and the new earth on her skin. He wanted her eyes to light up when she saw him coming with the same light that he had seen that afternoon. He wanted to hear her laugh.

The sky was now awash with pinks and purples as the sun sat just on the edge of his fields. Frankie sat on a small stool that had been placed in the midst of rows of rosemary and thyme.

He inhaled deeply, his fingers creating small furrows in the dirt. He began to hum, I *come to the garden alone* and a smile came from somewhere deep within and then there it was… amidst the confusion and the unrest there was one thing he knew for certain… that when Jaclyn had sung of peace, for the first time in a long time, Frankie had felt it…

Summer

Chapter twenty four

Rose dropped the kids off at camp and headed for Karilyne's Korner. Her stated purpose had been to deliver the wine Karilyne had ordered, but her true motive was that she hoped to meet the woman that Frankie was obviously in love with. Frankie never talked about the women he dated and Rose never pushed it, but this one was different... he had mentioned her name on more than one occasion. When Rose asked him about inviting her to dinner, Frankie had simply shaken his head and shrugged. He said she was beautiful, kind, talented and too good for someone like him.

"What do you mean too good for someone like you?!"

Frankie was frustrated with Rose's questions and even more frustrated with his own feelings. "I don't know... I mean I don't think I am the kind of man she would be interested in."

"You mean hard working? Passionate? Kind?" Rose was angry that anyone would think that Frankie wasn't a good man.

"It doesn't matter, Rose. I was stupid… I was obnoxious at best and I…" Frankie ran his fingers through his hair, remembering the last time he had spoken to Jaclyn, "I hurt her feelings and I don't know how to fix it." He threw his hands into the air, "Not even the endless charm of Francis Amante can fix this!"

Rose smiled, "Well, it sounds to me like this is a woman who needs wooing. Flowers… notes… candies. Not your usual bull in a china shop approach. "

Frankie shoved his hands into his pockets, "You mean tenderness? I've never tried that. Not sure I would have the slightest clue how to start."

Rose placed her hands on Frankie's shoulders and turned him towards the fields… the plants that he started from seed and gently coaxed into vibrant greens, reds, and yellows now awash with the gold from a late afternoon sun and whispered into the warm, spring air. "Yes, you do."

She parked in front of the cafe, grabbed the partitioned bag containing the bottles of whites and reds and walked to the back of the building. She knocked on the screen door and a voice coming from the garden called a hello. A woman with a basket of herbs walked towards her. "Can I help you?"

She was beautiful... her cheeks flushed with her morning's work in the garden and Rose wondered if this was the woman who had stolen Frankie's heart.

"Hello." Rose held up the bag of wine. "Yes, these are the bottles of wine from the farm. I had to take my kids to summer camp so I thought I would drop them off."

Karilyne frowned, "From the farm? Oh! You... you must be..."

"Joe's wife, Frankie's sister-in-law... and you must be..."

Karilyne blushed, wondering if Rose knew how stupidly she had acted. "Karilyne. I'm Karilyne."

Karilyne opened the screen door, "Thank you, please, come in."

Rose set the bag on the counter and took a deep breath, "Ah... cinnamon."

Karilyne grinned, "Yes... rolls to be exact, cinnamon rolls." She placed the basket of herbs next to the bag of wine, removed a large pan of bubbling rolls from the oven and stirred a bowlful of sweet, creamy goodness. She quickly spread the glaze over each roll and lifted one onto a plate. "Here."

"Really? Oh my... thank you."

Karilyne poured a glass of milk, "Let's go to the dining room so we can get you off your feet."

Karilyne sat quietly while Rose devoured the roll and milk. "Would you like another one?"

Rose shook her head as she swallowed the last

delicious bite, "Yes… I would love one but no… I don't need it! Thank you, though."

Karilyne smiled, "I remember those days… when are you due?"

Rose sighed, leaned back and patted her belly, "Six weeks… give or take."

"Boy or girl?"

"Don't know. We knew about the other three, but we wanted this one to be a surprise. It's funny, I insisted on knowing before, so that I could be prepared with clothes, colors, etc. and then by the time you get to the third one it doesn't matter… you're just dressing them in whatever is closest or cleanest!"

Karilyne laughed, "I had a boy and a girl. I bought a ton of blue for the first one and a ton of pink for the second one and as soon as she could choose…"

"Her favorite color was blue!"

"Of course."

Karilyne placed a pillow behind Rose's back. "It

must be difficult with your husband deployed."

"It would be if we didn't have Frankie. He fills in for Joe in every way he can. I think that's one of the reasons he hasn't found someone to settle down with... worried that he wouldn't be able to take care of us and his own family."

"I guess that's understandable." Karilyne was a little uncomfortable. She still wasn't sure if Frankie had told Rose about Karilyne's idiocy and, if so, if she had been sent to test the waters.

"Yes... but Joe is coming home for good this fall and now that Frankie has found someone I think he could really care about..."

Oh no... this is awkward.

"That is actually why I stopped by, the wine was an excuse. I was hoping to meet the woman that Frankie can't stop talking about."

Karilyne swallowed, folded her hands, placed them on the table and thought carefully about what to say. "Listen, Rose... I am very flattered by Frankie's adva…. ummm…. attention, but I am married…"

Rose shook her head and held up a hand but Karilyne continued, "and, yes, we are having some difficulties currently and apparently Frankie heard about my husbands extended business trip and thought that…well, it doesn't matter what he thought…anyway yes, we have some things to work out but…"

Rose knew she needed to stop Karilyne before she said something she didn't want Rose to know. She grabbed Karilyne's hands and shook her head, "No! It's… it's not you."

"Married couples do have problems, but we are…. *wait, what?* I'm sorry… what did you say?"

"You are not the woman Frankie is in….well, in love with."

Frankie… in love with… if not me then, who?

Karilyne frowned, "I think you might be at the wrong place. There are just three women working here. Me, Patricia and…"

"Jaclyn." Rose smiled, "Frankie's in love with Jaclyn."

Chapter Twenty five

"Karilyne, you know, you don't own sorrow. You don't have the tragedy market cornered." Patricia had been pushed to her limit. Another morning spent listening to Karilyne bemoaning her empty life had been the last straw. With every turn of the spoon, a heavy sigh. With every roll of the dough, a sharp word.

Karilyne sat stunned as Patricia continued.

"A lot of people lose things, including other people, but they don't sit on their asses waiting for a ghost to tell them how to live their lives! They simply get *off* their asses and figure out a way to put one foot in front of the other!"

"How can you say that after knowing what I have been through… losing my mother, my children and possibly my husband? How dare you! How could you possibly understand?!"

Patricia held up her hand. "Karilyne, people lose

their parents, it happens. Your children didn't die, they just had the nerve to grow up and if I was your husband, I would have gone a long time ago!" Patricia grabbed her bag from the counter and turned to leave when the contents fell onto the floor. Through tears of rage, she bent to scoop them up and place them back in her bag. "But quite frankly, I am sick of this conversation. I am tired of hearing about how tragic your life is and I am damned sick of being one of the people assigned to the task of constantly trying to cheer you up! You love self-pity so much...drown in it!"

The slamming door caused the small gold bell to ring for several moments before the silence enveloped the room. Karilyne sat with her arms crossed tightly against her body. Seething. Several minutes passed as she rocked, angrily. Eventually the rocking slowed along with her heartbeat. She stood, crossed the room, locked the café doors and turned to walk back to the kitchen. The late afternoon sun glinted off of a flat object lying just on the other side of the counter. Karilyne bent down and held in her hand two laminated cards. The first card was of Patricia in what appeared to be a photo of when she was around seven years old. Karilyne smiled, she hadn't changed much.

She turned the card over and her knees buckled. The obituary read *Anna, beloved daughter of Patricia and the late Peter*... Karilyne slid the second card from under the first. The picture of a handsome, young man followed by the words *Peter, loving husband and father died* the remaining words obliterated by Karilyne's tears. Tears of grief, but, mostly, tears of shame.

She sat on the café's wooden floor, clutching the cards to her chest "How could I not have known this? What sort of self-absorbed monster have I become?!"

What did she know about Patricia? What did she know about Jaclyn or Frankie or Kurt or herself for that matter? She had been so busy feeling sorry for herself that it had not occurred to her that any of it could possibly be her fault. She had no idea how she would make this up to Patricia. No idea how she was going to make it up to all of the other people she had ignored due to her own self-pity. She only knew she had to.

Chapter twenty six

The house was so quiet, just the faucet dripping and a clock ticking away precious minutes. Karilyne rummaged through the bathroom cabinet and found a bottle of Evening Rose bubble bath. She blew the dust from the top and poured two capfuls into the running water. It was supposed to have been a thoughtful gift from Jake and she thanked him for it and placed it in the back of the cabinet. She didn't care for roses. Her mother had been allergic to them so she preferred the scents of honeysuckle and lavender.

She watched the bubbles multiply and float, and when the tub was filled, she turned the faucet off, flipped the switch on a CD player, poured a glass of wine and lowered herself gingerly into the tub. She closed her eyes and listened as James Taylor returned to Carolina in his mind and breathed deeply.

Inhale red rose. Exhale blue mood. Inhale red rose.
Exhale blue mood.

She was struck by how much she liked the scent.
She closed her eyes and remembered when she had
been a little girl. Her mother had been diagnosed
with breast cancer at the age of twenty nine.
Karilyne was not allowed to visit her in the hospital
so her grandparents would drive slowly past the
huge, gray building and point to the window
beyond which her mother lay fighting.
Karilyne sank deeper into the tub and, as the water
covered her face, she remembered vividly the
afternoon that her father had returned home with
the single red rose her mother had sent to be
pressed into Karilyne's bible. Red, full, and
fragrant. "This was your mom's favorite, she
wanted you to have it." It remained pressed
between those pages, the bible safely tucked away
in the top of Karilyne's closet.

Wait a minute. That doesn't make any sense. *Why would you have roses in your room? You couldn't be anywhere near them because of your…*

Karilyne jolted upright in the tub, the scent of roses wafting about her damp hair and filling her nostrils. *You weren't. You were never allergic to roses.*

'Don't be afraid to stop and smell the roses' Grace had said.

Tears began to flow and mingle with the diminishing bubbles.

You didn't like having roses around because their scent reminded you of pain and fear. It was a lot easier just to say "no thank you, I'm allergic" than to have to relive the fear, the battle, and the scars.

Karilyne took a sip of wine and smiled. Her entire laugh flashed before her. All of the things she had missed out on, all of the chances she was too afraid to take. The fear that now that the children were grown and gone, Jake would leave as well.

When death came to call you looked him squarely in the

eye and said "no thank you, not today". But instead of instilling that strength in me, you instilled fear and uncertainty. A waiting for the next shoe to drop way of life. And today, for the first time…. I get it.

Karilyne's tears fell steady, heavy and… full of joy. This new knowledge gave her a sense of power she wasn't sure she had ever felt

Epiphanies come in small doses and in strange places and sometimes even in floating, rose-scented bubbles. She laughed when she thought of all of those hours spent at the lake looking for answers, looking for her mother and all the while, the answer had been tucked away in a forty year old bible.

Ok mom… time to get out of this tub and figure out how I am going to fix all of this. I have some fences to mend, wrongs to make right, a café to run, a life to live and most importantly, I have to get the love of my life back.

She started with a clean piece of paper, an ink pen, a fresh glass of wine and a phone call.

Rose was more than a little surprised when she

heard Karilyne's voice on the other end of the phone. The only time she had ever spoken with her was during their meeting at the cafe and, although she hadn't mentioned it to Frankie, she was under the impression that Karilyne was a little miffed that Frankie had been interested in Jaclyn and not her. But Karilyne's voice was warm when she asked Rose for her help.

The plan was simple. Rose was to make sure that Frankie was free on Saturday night. She would call and ask that he deliver a special order of mixed greens, his salad dressing, and a few bottles of wine to the café for a small, private party she was hosting. It would be Rose's job to insist that he go despite any protests.

Rose was skeptical, the last thing Frankie needed was to get mixed up with a married woman, "Then what?"

"Just leave the rest to me."

"The rest of what, Karilyne? I've already told you

that Frankie is interested in Jaclyn!"

It dawned on Karilyne that she hadn't divulged the entire plan. "Oh... no! Not for me. Jaclyn will be here waiting!"

"Ah, I see" Rose was beginning to understand and, more than that, she liked the plan. "Does Jaclyn know this?"

Karilyne laughed, "Absolutely not! There is no way I could get her here if she thought it was to have dinner with Frankie. I'll tell her I need help with the party."

Rose stood and looked out the kitchen window. She could see Frankie's outline in the dusk, working in the fields. "Gosh, Karilyne... I am going to keep my fingers crossed. It would mean so much if Frankie could settle down with a nice girl and have a family of his own."

Karilyne smiled, "I know. There is nothing like family. We have our work cut out for us. Dinner at seven... I will call you at five... that will give him just enough to time to pick the greens, mix the dressing and grab some wine."

"Got it! And don't worry, come hell or high water... he'll be there!"

Karilyne hung up and sat back in the wooden adirondack Jake had built when they had bought the house. Still wrapped in an oversized terry cloth robe, she tapped her pen against the pad of paper she had been so furiously making notes on.

Frankie and Jaclyn: dinner at café - salad, lasagna, ~~garlic~~ bread, one of patty's cheesecakes

Call Rose for help - tell Frankie I need greens, dressing and wine

Dinner at 7

Take Jaclyn shopping

Kurt and Patricia: Fourth of July picnic

Jake: Tell him you love him. Tell him you've been stupid. Tell him you've been selfish. Tell him you are willing to do whatever makes him happy. Remind him of your love... of your life together

Pray it's not too late.

Karilyne looked down at the doodle she had been mindlessly scribbling while watching the sky turn its dusk rainbow of pinks, blues, and purples. In between all of the notes, thoughts, hopes, and prayers she had drawn their gazebo.

Chapter twenty seven

Jaclyn paced nervously through the living room, occasionally checking for Karilyne's car. When Karilyne had first mentioned hosting small, private parties at the café, Jaclyn had been excited at the thought of being able to experiment with new ingredients and create personalized desserts for customers who would expect a unique dinner. Then Karilyne told her that she would be helping to serve... not just cook and Jaclyn, well.... had panicked.

"Please Karilyne... maybe Patty would want to help serve... I can just stay in the kitchen."

But Karilyne had insisted that Jaclyn spread her wings and become a bigger part of the business so, today, they were shopping for wings.

More specifically a dress, shoes, and Karilyne had said as an afterthought "maybe a new hairstyle and a little lipstick."

To be honest, Jaclyn wasn't sure if she was excited or afraid… or maybe… just maybe a little of both. The car's horn made her jump. She pushed her glasses back onto the tiny bridge of her nose, grabbed her backpack and headed out the door. Karilyne smiled as Jaclyn slid into the passenger seat. "Good morning."

"Good morning."

"Jaclyn… what is this?" Karilyne pointed to a red patch on her backpack.

Jaclyn bit her lower lip and looked sideways at Karilyne, "duct tape."

Karilyne nodded with approval, "Very resourceful" she had resolved that she would give no more negativity, "and the color matches your tennis shoes!"

Jaclyn grinned, "Thanks!"

Karilyne placed the car in reverse, "I hope you are ready for an adventure!"

Jaclyn thought for a minute. The last adventure she had was the day she had met Frankie and Patricia... so, yes... she was ready. "Full speed ahead!"

Their first stop was Laura's Lingerie shop. Karilyne, Laura and her sister Lynda had all gone to school together. When the majority of their class had gone off to college, the girls stayed behind, secured a bank loan for a dilapidated building in the city and had transformed it into a lingerie and dress shop. It had been a surprise to everyone in the village. The sisters had always been sort of tomboys... not one person could recall a day when they had seen either of them in a dress except on graduation day. It had been an even bigger surprise when the shop was a success. Laura was a 'little rough around the edges' but she knew what she was doing. She had already assembled several sets of lingerie based on the information Karilyne had given her. *She is tall, slim and, I think, hidden underneath layers of baggy t-shirts, stained aprons and over-sized jeans, there is a nice figure.*

Your job is to find it. Not a problem… that was precisely what Laura's shop was all about.

An eager Karilyne and a reluctant Jaclyn entered the shop promptly at nine. Laura emerged from the shop's office when she heard the door. "Good morning, Karilyne… so good to see you and this must be Jaclyn."

"Good morning Laura, thanks for the appointment and yes, this is…"

"Turn around." Laura motioned for Jaclyn to turn. She stood with her hands on her hips, clucking her tongue, her head cocked to one side sizing up her assignment. "What… what is this you are wearing, sweetheart."

Jaclyn shot Karilyne a worried glance.

"Overalls… they are overalls. It's what Jaclyn normally wears to work, but we are hosting a party this evening and we knew you and Lynda could give Jaclyn a fresh look." Karilyne turned away from Jaclyn and gave Laura a look that said 'be gentle'.

Laura smiled, "Well, that's understandable. They look like very comfortable work clothes, but I agree with Karilyne... might be time for a change." Laura took Jaclyn by the hand, "Come with me."

Karilyne took a seat just outside the dressing room and held her breath.

"Wait... what?" Jaclyn's voice a high wail from inside the room.

"It's ok, Jaclyn. She just needs to get your measurements."

"But she wants me to take my...my..."

"Oh my, Karilyne. This has got to be the tightest sport bra I have ever seen! You got this when you were what... twelve?"

Jaclyn's voice now defiant, "No! And they have to be tight otherwise... my... *they...* bounce around when I ride my bike!"

Karilyne stifled a laugh. "I understand, honey, but wouldn't it be nice to have some pretty new things?"

"I guess."

"So, close your eyes, take a deep breath and let Laura do her job."

There was a moment of silence and then the dressing room door opened. A triumphant Laura walked past Karilyne, "Guess who has breasts?" Jaclyn stood in the dressing room clutching her shirt to her bare torso. She looked into the mirror and brushed the hair from her face. She couldn't remember the last time she had looked at herself in a mirror other than the small one above her bathroom sink. It hadn't been necessary... she wore the same thing every day... she knew what she looked like... or did she. *Ok... one... two... three.* She let the t-shirt fall to the dressing room floor, straightened her shoulders, looked into the mirror and smiled. She remembered the hours she had spent lying on her mother's bed while she dressed in front of the mahogany full-length mirror that stood in her bedroom. She wanted to look just like her... curvy... voluptuous... but instead she had simply continued to grow taller and thinner and had stopped paying attention to what she looked like under the layers of cotton and denim. She realized now that she looked like her dad's mother and, more than that, for the very first time, she knew it was ok. *Beautiful. Maybe it's time to stop selling yourself short. Maybe it's time to start thinking about your future... the one that dad wanted for you. Maybe it's time to grab the ring and start living the life you deserve.*

Laura's voice broke the silence, "Are you ready in there?"

Jaclyn took a deep breath, looked into the mirror and nodded at her reflection, "Yes... I'm ready."

The next hour was spent dressing Jaclyn in a variety of lingerie... practical white 'bicycle bras' and panties and pretty, colored satin and lace.

Laura cleared the dressing room of all but one set.

272

"Put those on, you'll need to wear them while you shop for your dress."

Jaclyn obediently put on a lavender demi-bra and hi-cut lace panties. "Excuse me... where are my clothes?"

Laura tossed a terry cloth robe with the boutique's name embroidered on the left breast over the dressing room door. "Just wear the robe... you are only going next door to my sister's." She glanced at the trash can by the back door, "don't worry... I'll take care of your clothes."

The next two hours were spent trying on what felt to Jaclyn like every dress in the store. Below the knee... above the knee... mid-thigh and no way skirt lengths. Scoop neck... boat neck... v neck and absolutely not necklines. Karilyne suggested that it might be too early in the game for cleavage. Lynda shrugged, "Whatever you say, but if I had that body I would be showing it off!"

"Yes... I know. You don't and yet you do!"

Lynda's ample bosom jiggled with her laughter. "Ok... I think I have the perfect dress for tonight!" She was right. Jaclyn was breathtaking in a simple light blue sheath gathered on either side of the waist with small buckles and a white sweater with light blue trim at the neck and the wrists.

Karilyne stood behind her as she studied her reflection in a full length mirror. "It's perfect, Jaclyn. You look beautiful."

Jaclyn smiled and felt the sting of joyful tears, "I do... don't I?"

Lynda called from the other side of the shop, "You need shoes!"

They glanced down at Jaclyn's red sneakers, "Coming!"

Jaclyn had only worn a pair of heels twice in her life...her graduation and her father's funeral. She reasoned with Karilyne that her first night of serving new customers was not the ideal time to learn to balance in heels. Karilyne smiled and agreed… Jaclyn, of course, didn't know she wouldn't be serving anything. They decided on a pair of white sling-backs with a small heel and small, white clutch with a silver buckle that matched those on the dress.

"I won't use it… I have a perfectly good backpack…"

Karilyne laughed, "You mean the one being held together by duct tape?"

Jaclyn shrugged, "Ok… I'll take the purse."

Karilyne made mental check marks next to her list:

Pick up Jaclyn - check

Laura's for underwear - check

Lynda's for dress - check

Jeanette's for hair and makeup

Glasses to go for contacts

They left Lynda's with four dresses including the blue sheath Jaclyn was wearing. Karilyne explained to her that there would not be enough time to change.

At Jeanette's, Karilyne and Jeanette conferred while Jaclyn swiveled in the padded, chrome chair. "Not too much change, just trim the split ends and shape it up." Karilyne didn't want to change the girl that Frankie had fallen in love with but she did want him to see the woman hidden behind the denim and the tattered apron strings she used in her hair. "Ok... we are going to start with a shampoo, then a cut and a little styling."

Jaclyn held up her hand, "Not too much... tell her Karilyne. I have to be able to pull it back into a ponytail for work. Tell her Karilyne... it has to be pulled back while I am in the kitchen."

Karilyne placed her hands on Jaclyn' shoulders and turned her towards the salon's mirror. "Haven't things gone well so far today?"

Jaclyn nodded.

"Then trust me... Jeanette knows what she is doing."

Jaclyn took a deep breath… "Ok."

Karilyne stepped outside and sent a message to Rose's phone.

Everything going well here… how bout there?

It took only a matter of seconds before her phone buzzed.

So far so good. He thinks he is staying here this evening… pizza and a movie with the boys… don't worry… he'll be there… with bells on!!

Karilyne chuckled. Bells or no bells…he was in for a night he wasn't going to forget.

Within an hour, Jaclyn's waves had been transformed into beautiful, soft layers that framed her face. Jeanette had coaxed her into a little blush, mascara and a light pink lip color and packed a small cosmetic bag that fit into the clutch.

She turned the chair towards Karilyne, "Well? What do you think?"

Karilyne was speechless. All of these months… this small, frail, flour covered girl was actually a tall, shapely, beautiful, young woman.

"Karilyne… is it ok?"

Karilyne nodded. "It's better than ok… it's beautiful. He's going to love it."

Jaclyn smiled, "Wait… what? Who's going to love it?"

Karilyne stammered, realizing that she had spoken out loud. "I meant they… the clients are going to love it… you know… because you look like a professional hostess."

Jaclyn beamed, "Really?"

Karilyne nodded, "Yes, really. Now, I am starving and we probably won't be eating until after the dinner so let's go to the Bunny Hutch and get a salad."

Jaclyn frowned, "Are you sure? The last time I was there it wasn't very good."

"Yes, I know, but they have changed their supplier. They are getting their produce from the same guy that supplies us… you know…," Karilyne snapped her fingers, "what's his name."

Jaclyn blushed and traced the buckle on the clutch, "Frankie... you mean Frankie."

Karilyne feigned remembering, "Oh! That's right... Frankie. I had forgotten his name."

Maybe you have but I haven't. I say his name every morning as I mix the dough and every afternoon as I pick the herbs and every night as I lay in bed. Frankie... Frankie. How could you possibly forget?

Karilyne thought it might be a good idea for Jaclyn to break in her new shoes so they left the car at the salon and walked the three blocks to the Bunny Hutch.

A gentle breeze rustled the outdoor tables' brightly, colored umbrellas. Karilyne assured Jaclyn that it wasn't 'too windy' for her new hair style. They sipped on iced ginger/peach tea while waiting for their salads.

Jaclyn laid one napkin across her lap, tucked another one into the neck of her new dress, and shoved her glasses back onto her nose.

Glasses- to -go for contacts

Karilyne cleared her throat, "Umm... I was thinking that maybe, after lunch, we might have enough time to stop by the glasses-to-go place and get some contacts or maybe a new pair of glasses."

Jaclyn's hands flew to either side of the oversized frames.

Karilyne continued, "I mean, I don't know what the prescription is but it is possible that they might have something that they could fit you with immediately or within the hour."

Jaclyn lowered her eyes and folded her hands in her lap, "There is no prescription."

Karilyne sat her tea glass on the table, "I'm sorry... what?"

Jaclyn continued softly, "There is no prescription... they were my dad's. I had the lenses replaced with plastic."

Karilyne sighed, "I understand..."

Jaclyn raised her chin and shook her head, "No you don't. You think it's childish and silly and maybe you're right, but wearing them makes me feel like he is with me."

"Jaclyn... wait." Karilyne reached into her blouse and pulled on a small silver chain. "Look."

Jaclyn leaned forward and held the locket in her palm, "It's a cameo."

Karilyne nodded, "Yes. It is a tarnished, chipped, worn-out cameo. It was my mother's... so I can't possibly tell you that wearing your dad's glasses is silly or childish because I completely understand hanging on to memories."

Karilyne reached behind her neck, opened the chain's clasp, placed it on the table between the two of them and reached for Jaclyn's hand. "There are no time limits on missing someone, but maybe there should be on simply living to miss them."

"It's time I realized that my mom doesn't exist in an old locket around my neck and your dad is not in a pair of frames on the bridge of your perfect nose."

Jaclyn thought for several moments, then slid the frames from her face and placed them on the table next to Karilyne's cameo.

"I don't have to throw them away, do I?"

"No... absolutely not. I'll tell you what we'll do, we will put them in a memory box and keep it at the café and any time we want to see them, they'll be there."

"Agreed?"

Jaclyn smiled, "Agreed."

The salads arrived and while Jaclyn chatted with the waitress, Karilyne dropped the glasses and the chain into her bag.

The sun's position reminded her of the day's plan and she checked her watch, *we have just enough time to eat, get to the café, set the table, prepare the food and wait...*

Frankie stood next to Rose at the kitchen sink as she

strained to see something in the distance. "What are you looking for?"

Rose jumped, "Oh! God… Frankie you scared me. I… I didn't hear you come in."

Frankie took a large gulp of tea, "Sorry, Rose. You lookin' for the boys?"

"No, actually… I was looking for you. That woman called from that café and…"

Frankie held up a hand, "Wait… slow down. What woman and what café?"

Okay Rose… calm down… this has to be convincing.

"Um… Karilyne… her name was Karilyne and she is hosting a private party at the café tonight and needs some mixed greens, some vinaigrette and some wine."

Frankie shrugged and poured another glass of tea, "Too bad… I promised the boys star wars and pepperoni tonight… she'll have to call somebody else."

"There will be plenty of time for a movie and pizza

and it sounded like she was desperate."

Frankie sighed, "So what exactly did she say?"

I think I have him. "Apparently someone called and asked if he could have the café for a private dinner and she thought it would be a good idea to start hosting private events."

"Alright... I'll drop the stuff off, pick up the pizza and be back within the hour."

Rose shook her head, "There's no rush. You have time to get everything ready, shower..."

"I don't need a shower... I'm gonna walk in the back door, lay the stuff on the counter and come back!"

"No!"

"What?!"

Calm down Rose. "It sounds like these might be the kind of people who are interested in wine. I think you should at least do a shirt and tie and take a business card... don't give me that look," Rose placed her hands on her belly, "after all, we're going to need the money."

Frankie smiled, "Very good, Rose… the mommy guilt card… okay, you win."

"Good… so you got it? Greens, dressing, wine, shirt, tie, business card and bouquet."

"Yeah… got it… wait… bouquet?"
"Yes, please… it will give you the chance to extend an invitation to visit the garden and the winery."

Frankie sighed, "Not the evening I had planned… tell the boys, I'll be back in plenty of time."

Rose nodded as she shoved Frankie towards the back door, "Don't worry, I will and wear the new blue shirt I got you for Christmas."

"Okay… okay." There was no reason to argue… he knew when he was beat and he also knew Rose was right… things were going well for the farm, but it would be a huge boost for them if people began to come to them for wine.

He walked slowly with a harvest basket, carefully picking a mix of salad greens. He paused and looked out over the fields. He pictured Jaclyn there, kneeling, planting and singing just as she had in the small café garden. The wind blowing through her hair and the sun warming her cheeks. He rounded the barn and followed the path to the winery, picturing Jaclyn along the way. He chose several bottles of wine, the same variety he had served Karilyne when she had visited the farm. *Karilyne... hopefully she'll be too busy to talk.* He had managed to avoid having conversations with her since that day and had made several awkward attempts to strike up a conversation with Jaclyn, but was always interrupted by Karilyne, Patricia or an oven timer. Every night before he went to bed, he held his phone in his hand, willing himself to call the number he'd found in an old phone book, but couldn't bring himself to dial. If she answered... what would he say? For the first time in his life... he was afraid of a woman's rejection... *not just a woman... Jaclyn.*

He cut a basket full of his favorite flowers and tied them into a bouquet using grapevine twine. He checked his watch… he had just enough time to shower, dress and get to the café before the dinner.

The lasagna was in the oven. Karilyne had followed Rose's recipe to the letter… *it's his favorite.* She had Jaclyn busy preparing an antipasto platter while she set the table and placed a Sinatra CD in the player she had moved to the dining room. She glanced nervously between the table setting and the front window waiting for Frankie's van to appear. She lit the candles, moved the wine glasses for the tenth time and checked the clock. *Calm down… he's not late.* She walked back to the kitchen to check on Jaclyn's progress.

Frankie stopped the van just short of the café leaving the space directly in front for guests. He decided to carry the wine and flowers into the dining room and let Karilyne choose the mix she wanted from the back of the van.

The bell above the door jingled and Karilyne jumped. Jaclyn frowned, "Are you okay? It sounds like the guests have arrived."

"Yes… you're right… it sounds like they are here. Um… I will check the lasagna and you go and greet them."

"No! You should do that… I still have," Jaclyn looked helplessly around the room, "something to do…"

Karilyne shook her head, "No you don't, I think your tray looks perfect, now go on." Karilyne untied the apron Jaclyn wore over the new dress and gently shoved her towards the door. Jaclyn took a deep breath, smoothed the front of her dress, placed her hand on the door and glanced back at Karilyne. "Go ahead… you look beautiful."

Jaclyn walked into the dining room, smiled and began to extend her hand, but when the man holding the bouquet turned towards her, her hand instinctively covered her rapidly beating heart.

Frankie turned, expecting to find Karilyne. He stood looking at the young woman who had only weeks before been the girl in the garden. Neither of them spoke for several moments and then, finally, Frankie realized that this dinner was for them. There were no clients coming... the special guests were him... and Jaclyn.

He became aware of the flowers he still held in his hand... the flowers that he had picked while all the time wishing Jaclyn were there to see them,

"Here... these are for you."

Jaclyn blushed and accepted the bouquet, "They are beautiful... thank you."

"Not as beautiful as you."

Karilyne walked into the dining room, pushed the button on the CD player and walked softly towards the door. She began to remind them that the lasagna was in the oven and the bread needed to go in as soon as the lasagna came out, but the two were slowly swaying as Sinatra sang... *someday when I'm awfully low...just the way you look tonight* she opened the door and walked out into the warm evening air. She turned to walk to her car, but paused for just a moment, looked back through the window at the glow cast from the candles and theirs smiles and, for the first time in a long time, she felt the stirring of life's possibilities.

Chapter twenty eight

Karilyne had taken gloves and a scraper to the pond. She was determined to put a fresh coat of paint on the bench's rusted hummingbirds. She scraped and peeled and took note of those places that would require filler before she could paint. The ducks dove deeply into the newly stocked pond, reveling in their precious finds.

After an hour or so of squatting, bending and scraping, she sat to rest. She sat back and closed her eyes, the sun warming her cheeks when she felt someone sit next to her. She turned and through squinted eyes, saw Patricia's beautiful smile. Patricia placed her hand on Karilyne's, "I'm sorry." "No… don't." Karilyne stammered and searched for words. "I'm… I'm the one that should be apologizing." She reached into her pocket and retrieved the cards. "Here, you dropped these." Patricia took the cards, pressed them to her breast and smiled. "They were beautiful weren't they?"

"She looked just like you." Karilyne paused for a moment. "I'm so sorry. How could I not have known about this?"

Patricia sat for a moment, watching the ducks dip, "you never asked."

"How....?" Karilyne's voice a whisper.

"A drunk driver hit them on the way to a father-daughter dance."

Oh God! Karilyne thought. *There are no words for this.*

"I'm so sorry… you should have told me. I can't imagine how hard it's been to keep that inside."

Patricia's lips quivered, she fought to control her voice as she tried to say something that she had yet to say out loud. "It… it was my fault."

Karilyne's heart skipped a beat. "How? You… Patty… you weren't driving?"

"No… I was home."

Karilyne placed her hand on Patricia's back, "I don't understand… then how can it have been your fault?"

"I left the camera upstairs."

Karilyne frowned and shook her head.

"They were hit within minutes of leaving the house. If I had placed the camera on the hall table. If I hadn't had to go upstairs. If I hadn't...."

"Oh Patty. You can't possibly know what happened after they left the house. So many things... traffic lights... a dog running in front of the car... so many things that could have changed their route."

Patricia buried her face into her hands, "Stop... you're being logical. It doesn't matter what else might have happened... my heart aches every day from what I didn't do."

"Like what...?"

"I didn't plan... I didn't pay attention to the time. He may have been hurrying because I kept them for those extra minutes. I... I," Patricia sobbed into her hands, her deep breaths rocking her body, "I didn't protect them... I didn't save them!"

They sat in silence for several minutes, Karilyne knowing that she didn't have the words to erase the guilt that her friend carried. "Did you get to see them?"

"Anna died at the scene of the accident in Peter's arms. Peter died a few hours later at the hospital. His last words were 'promise me you'll take care of my little one'." Patricia continued through choking sobs, "My little one…that's what he called her. He didn't know I was never going to be able to keep the promise. He didn't know his little one… *our precious little one was gone!*"

Patricia sank into Karilyne's arms. Karilyne held her tightly and let her cry. She bit her tongue when she began to say that it was going to be alright… she knew better… it was never going to be alright. Patricia took a deep breath, wiped the tears from her face and leaned back on the bench.

Karilyne thought about the last few months, the time since Patty had become part of the daily life at

the Korner. "How did you get through it? I mean...
it has been your attitude and your smiles that have
gotten me through a lot of crummy days the past
few months. How do you manage to go on?"

"I read a letter."

"Someone sent you a letter?"

"Sort of. I purchased a book of letters at the St.
James library book sale. I couldn't have told you
why then until I opened to a random page and
read... this." Patricia handed a carefully folded
piece of paper.

Karilyne read, in silence, a beautiful love letter
written by someone who was obviously deeply in
love with not only her husband but with life. She
spoke of the richness of life and the blessings she
had known with him. Karilyne folded the paper
and handed it back to Patricia. "It's beautiful,
but..."

"It was written by Anne Morrow Lindbergh to her
husband Charles."

"She really loved him."

"Yes, she did…. as much as I loved Peter and… as much as you love Jake."

Karilyne nodded and smiled. "So much happiness followed by so much sorrow. Is that it… the letter means so much because you know what it's like to lose your happiness in a second?"

Patricia shook her head. "It wasn't the letter that changed my life, it was the date on the letter. It was written in 1944. Their baby had been abducted and murdered in 1932. I don't know exactly what Anne did immediately after the loss of her child. I am sure she did what the rest of us do when we are grieving. Renounce God. Curl up in a ball. Cry. Scream. Blame others, blame ourselves. Hide. But what struck me was that at some time or another she stopped crying, stopped blaming, stopped hiding and decided instead to embrace what life had given instead of what it had taken."

"You make it sound so easy."

"No, not easy… necessary. I am sure that she felt just as guilty about the death of her son as I felt about the deaths of Peter and Anna."

"She couldn't have done anything about a horrible human being who chose to murder her baby any more than you could about a horrible drunk driver!"

"It doesn't work that way… you know that. Think of all of the times that you blamed yourself for your mother's death even though, rationally, you must know it isn't true."

Karilyne looked out over the lake and thought of all of the time she had spent wondering if she had only been more aware, paid more attention…

"But that's different…"

Patricia smiled and placed the letter and the cards into her bag. "No… it's not. I blamed myself because I left the camera upstairs and they were killed within minutes of leaving. If only I had been better prepared… if only the camera had been near the front door... if only I hadn't fixed her bow... if only I hadn't straightened his tie... if only... if only... But if Anne could endure it and live a life filled with love and gratitude, then maybe I can too."

Karilyne smiled, "I guess it is time to start living with the fact that she is gone and my husband and my kids and..." she took Patricia's hand in hers, "my friends... are still here."

"You are such an idiot!"

"Gee, thanks..."

"I'm sorry, but for someone who is so smart you can be so stupid sometimes! Your mother is all around you Karilyne. She is in the ivy that surrounds the café door. She is in the eyes of the elderly couple that you never charge and have somehow managed to convince that they won a weekly free lunch. She is in the songs that your mother sang to you and, if you would stop for just one moment, instead of sitting here morning after morning waiting to feel her touch, you would realize that her hand is on yours every day when you stir the soups that she and Grace taught you to make."

They sat together, hands clasped, basking in the sun... tears of joy and friendship.

"I have had a pathetic, self-pitying year. But I promise, I am going to make it up to you... to everyone I have ignored or hurt."

Patricia shook her head, "No need."

Karilyne was insistent, "I want to... really."

Patricia shrugged, "Ok... but maybe later because, of course you realize that as we sit here... Jaclyn is in charge!"

"Oh God... you're right! Today's Special: Varnished Veggies!"

The two friends stood and began the walk up the trail. "Hey Patty, maybe you can teach me how to make those spice cakes that everyone raves about."

"No way!"

"What do you mean… no way?"

"I mean that is my family's recipe and I was sworn to secrecy!"

"Oh come on… I won't tell anybody… we're family!"

The chalk board in front of the café stated the day's menu.

Tuna salad

Chicken salad

Potato salad

Pasta salad

Key lime cheesecake

Mocha brownies with vanilla bean ice cream

Karilyne and Patricia stood looking at the board. They spoke simultaneously, "Did you plan this?"

"No."

"No."

"Jaclyn?"

Jaclyn heard the voices and hollered from the

kitchen. "Hey, you two… get in here, we have work to do!"

The two friends looked at each other, a mix of curiosity and fear on each face.

Jaclyn stood in the middle of the small kitchen with a paper and pen calling off a list of ingredients as an aproned Frankie retrieved each one.

Karilyne and Patricia stood motionless… their arms at their sides and their chins on their chests. As soon as she was satisfied with the neatly placed checks next to each item on the list she turned to the speechless pair.

"Ok… you two need to get busy. I have promised delivery of four hundred fruit hand pies to the 4th of July food tent and they are not going to make themselves."

Karilyne and Patricia stood cemented to the hardwood floor and, when they didn't budge, Jaclyn snapped her fingers in front of their faces.

"Hey! You two… did you hear me?"

Patricia glanced at Karilyne. "What is happening?!"

Jaclyn had taken Frankie's hand and they were headed out the back door. "We'll be back in a while."

"Wait! Where are you two going?"

Jaclyn rolled her eyes, "Berry picking...duh!"

Frankie smiled sheepishly and shrugged. "Berry picking!"

Jaclyn called over her shoulder from the garden, "Make enough dough for four mixed berry tarts with lemon cream.... those will be our center pieces."

Karilyne watched the two drive off in Frankie's van and turned back to find Patricia stunned and stammering. "What... I... you... *Frankie...* was that Jaclyn!?"

Karilyne nodded and tried to speak through the laughter that had doubled her over.

Chapter twenty nine

Karilyne dressed in a simple, red, cotton dress, white sneakers and knotted a blue, plaid kerchief around her neck. She checked herself in the hall mirror and saw something she had been missing for quite a while... her smile. Jake had called and said he was on his way home. He gave no specifics but said he was driving rather than flying and ended with the words that Karilyne had been mulling all week... *we need to talk.* She closed her eyes and imagined his voice over and over... had his tone been hopeful or ominous... she couldn't be sure but she refused to think anything but positive thoughts. Watching Jaclyn and Frankie had reminded her of the first days her and Jake had been in love... she wanted that back. She checked her watch and reminded herself that although this would be the first Fourth of July that she would spend without Jake, today wasn't about her... it was about Kurt...

and Patricia.

She had, once again, enlisted help but this time it wasn't Rose… it was Kurt's daughters. They had met Patricia at the café and they agreed with Karilyne… she would be perfect for their dad… now they just needed the perfect setting to plant a seed and the fourth of July picnic was the place. She grabbed a large tote with a sailboat motif, checked its contents; sweater, sunscreen, lipstick, sunglasses and wine and headed out the door. Jaclyn and Frankie would be waiting for her at the café to load 400 carefully crafted berry hand pies and four berry tart centerpieces. She had called ahead to make certain that the tables had been placed under the shade of the tent and on the opposite of the girl scouts bake sale, so no hard choices would have to be made and, as the day passed, the villagers would be certain to visit both. Jaclyn and Frankie had loaded the pies into several large bins with adjustable shelving so all that was left was to load them into the van. Karilyne placed the larger tarts into individual pie baskets in her trunk, made a quick call to Patricia to make sure she was on the way and the three set out for the day-long celebration.

As magical and holy as the village made Christmas, the Fourth of July was equal in its patriotism. The porches of the older homes were draped with red, white and blue bunting. Commander Dodd from the local VFW woke at sunrise to raise the flag that stood at the north end of the village square and the festivities were kicked off with a gathering and prayer at the small, war memorial that had been placed within a few feet of the flag, a tribute to those men and women who had left the warmth and safety of the village to serve their country.

Each room at Mrs. Richard's bed and breakfast was booked. Angie had been urged for years to create a website to bring customers to the oldest home in the village but it had never been necessary…. people came. Allert Village wasn't the place to visit if you were looking for shopping, major museums or theater, but it was the perfect place to visit if you wanted to spend a quiet weekend in an old Victorian with a fireplace and a basket of fresh muffins in your room. At Angie's, you would wake up to the smell of bacon, sausages, cinnamon and fresh coffee. After breakfast, a walk on the trails that wrapped around the village and the lake, and a visit to the small museum that had been created in an old train boxcar where you would find the village history and photos. Lunch at Karilyne's Korner, a nap in an over-sized four-poster bed and dinner at Angie's... fried chicken, potato salad, corn on the cob and banana cream pie. A weekend in Allert village was for relaxing as the cross-stitch sampler that hung just above the oak buffet in Angie's dining room stated

Welcome to Allert Village

where we count our blessings

The van and Karilyne's car drove slowly through
the village, waving to neighbors and allowing the
boy scouts to zig-zag the streets placing small,
wooden flags into the lawn of every home.

Mr. Vandyke had Molly hooked up to a large, red,
hay-filled wagon ready to take residents and
visitors alike through and around the village. The
day's events included a dunk tank, a baseball game,
a fishing and hot dog eating contest, a band concert
and of course, fireworks at dusk.

Officer Edwards cleared the way for Frankie to
back the van up to the waiting, shaded tables.
Karilyne parked in the nearby lot and joined the
two and insisted to not even a slight protest, "You
guys go have fun...I've got this!"

Jaclyn grabbed a basket and a blanket from the
front seat, "Okay... we'll see you in a while... just
buzz if you need help!"

Karilyne laughed as she watched the two of them walking hand in hand towards the less crowded end of the lake. She opened the back of the van and began to unload the pies when a second pair of hands reached for a tray, "Can I give you a hand?" Karilyne turned to find a familiar face, "Yes… thanks. Oh gosh! Ruth! How are you?" The woman who had spent Christmas Eve at St. James… her first Christmas without her mother. "I'm doing well… how about you?"

"I'm good."

The two continued to unload tray after tray of pies until the back of the van was empty and the tables were overflowing. The pies were carefully arranged, leaving two places on each table to accommodate the tart centerpieces.

"Last time we spoke I thought you were going back to St. Louis."

Ruth nodded, "I was going to until I spent some time in the village and I didn't want to leave. There

308

has been just enough money after the sale of the house to put a down payment on a little shack on the edge of town… just enough room for me and the cat!"

"That's wonderful… if you need anything for the house I am sure I can help you find it."

"Thank you… I might take you up on that."

"What about a job, Ruth… didn't you leave a job in St. Louis?"

"Yes, I did and to be honest, I wasn't sure what I was going to do and then Father O'Brien called and asked if I would be interested in being the church secretary… Mrs. Collins is retiring so I jumped at the chance."

Karilyne smiled, "That's right… well, I can't think of a better person to fill her shoes."

Ruth laughed, "I hope so… I've never been a secretary… I'm gonna wing it."

"I had never owned a café but it's going pretty well… you'll be just fine."

Ruth looked towards the cheers that came from the village baseball diamond, "If you don't need any more help, I think I'll go watch the game."

Karilyne shook her head, "No, I have recruited help so go enjoy yourself." Ruth turned to walk away when Karilyne stopped her, "Ruth, I wanted to thank you for our talk on Christmas Eve. I didn't realize until recently how much it really meant."

Ruth smiled and shrugged, "Just two women missing their mothers and trying to get through the holiday without them."

"Yes... but we weren't... were we?"

"Without them?" Ruth reached for Karilyne's hand, "not for one minute."

Patricia was waiting at the tables when Karilyne arrived with the baskets from her trunk. "Well, look who is here after all of the work has been done!" Patricia shook her head and took a long drink from a water bottle, "That clunker wouldn't start... I had to ride my bike and what do you mean 'all the work' I think making the dough for 400 hand pies is a little bit of work!" Karilyne laughed, "Oh! That's right... you did do that."

The two placed the tarts in their designated places in the midst of all of the pies, stepped back and admired their work.

"You rode your bike all the way from the Andres farm?"

Patricia nodded while finishing the water.

"Why didn't you call me?"

Patricia's eyes narrowed, "I did."

Karilyne checked her phone; Missed call from Patty, "Oh... sorry."

"Quite alright." Patricia tossed her bottle into a recycling bin. "So... who has the first shift... you or me?"

"Neither... let's go have some fun and I'll leave the honor jar on the table for now."

Karilyne placed an extra-large mason jar with the words Hand pies - $3 each... Thank you! on each table. "That'll do... now let's go find the rest of the crew."

They walked towards the festivities, "Frankie and Jaclyn are all the way down there, around the bend and Kurt and the girls are on the other side of the lake... should we walk or take a paddle boat?"

Patricia clapped her hands, "Oooo... let's paddle!"

The two friends paddled slowly, letting the cool water splash their legs and faces. They maneuvered their way through the other paddle boats and made certain to avoid the part of the lake where groups of four had cast their lines and were patiently waiting for 'the big one' to swallow their hooks.

They reached the opposite side of the lake and surrendered their boat to a waiting couple. A short walk and they found Kurt, Shannon and Brigitte eating snow cones on a red, white and blue quilt. "Looks like you guys are embracing the spirit of the day!"

Kurt spoke through a mouth full of ice,

"Absolutely!"

The girls jumped to hug Karilyne and Patricia.

"We've been waiting for you!"

"We've been working."

The girls protested in unison, "Not all of it... you promised we could sell pies!"

Karilyne laughed and took a bite from Shannon's cherry flavored cone, "Well, golly... if you insist."

Kurt cleared a wicker basket and various sweatshirts from the blanket and offered seats to Karilyne and Patricia. Karilyne sat first making sure that the spot next to Kurt was left for Patricia. The group sat quietly for a few minutes watching the storybook scene before them... the paddle boats, the gleeful squeals from the dunk tank as the mayor was suddenly dropped into the tepid water, the ice cream truck, the hot dogs, scout troops... all underneath a cloudless July sky.

The girls broke the silence, each grabbing an arm, "C'mon, Karilyne... let's go!"

"Alright... alright... I'm coming!" Patricia lifted her hand to her forehead to shield her eyes from the summer sun, "You need me?"

Karilyne shook her head, "No... you have absolutely, positively done enough. Stay right here and see if Kurt managed to pack anything worth eating in that basket... we'll be back in a while."

Kurt looked indignant, "I beg your pardon.... I..."

"Don't worry, Patty... Grandma packed the basket!"

Patricia smiled and glanced at Kurt, "Busted."

Kurt nodded and shrugged, "The downside of living with a couple of *blabbermouths*... impossible to lie!"

Karilyne and the girls were already walking, well on their way back to the lake trail... giggling and giving each other thumbs up.

The afternoon flew by... Karilyne and the girls selling pies and chatting with what seemed to be the entire village. They invited all newcomers to lunch at the café and reminded the regulars to stop by for their favorite soup and pastries.

By late afternoon, the pies were gone, the tarts had been delivered to St. James and the bins were loaded into the van when Karilyne's phone rang. The sun's glare prevented her from reading the name, she answered, expecting to hear Patricia's voice on the other end.

"Hello?"

"Karilyne..."

Karilyne's heart skipped a beat, "Jake... Jake, where are you?"

"Home... I'm home Karilyne."

Chapter thirty

It took Karilyne half an hour to find the owner of the car that had blocked her in and, once she was able to leave the parking lot, she was still forced to drive slowly through the village avoiding Fourth of July revelers and then following Mr. Vandyke and Molly for at least a mile. The minute she reached the outskirts of town, she stomped on the gas pedal, slowing only at the top of suicide hill and then stopping at the bottom. *Please, God… give me the right words to make this work. Help me make Jake understand how much he means to me… how much our love means to me… how much we have to look forward to.* She placed the car back in gear and drove slowly to the house.

The smile she had seen in the rear view mirror after hearing Jake's voice quickly disappeared as she approached the drive. A moving van was backed up to the rear of the house. Karilyne pulled into the circle and ran up the stairs, flung open the door and called for Jake. His suitcases sat in the hallway. She ran up the stairs and from room to room… down the stairs, through the living room and the dining room. She opened the basement door and called again, "Jake!"

"Karilyne…"

She turned and threw herself into Jake's arms, "Don't go… please don't go! I've been stupid and selfish and I… *I have missed you so much!*"

Jake held Karilyne tightly, "Karilyne… I'm not going anywhere."

Karilyne wiped the tears from her cheeks, "But there's a moving van in the drive… I just assumed…"

Jake smiled, "Close your eyes and come with me."

Karilyne frowned, "Where are we going?"

"Karilyne… do you trust me?"

Karilyne nodded, "Implicitly."

"Then close your eyes and hold my hand."

He led her through the kitchen, the breakfast nook, out the back door, down the deck stairs and across the lawn, "Now... open."

It was an exact replica. The place where they had fallen in love...where they had been married...where they had taken their kids to picnic when they had been small...their gazebo.

Karilyne began to cry again, "It's... it... I... I love it... it's *perfect...*"

"Come on... there's more."

They walked hand in hand to the gazebo as Jake explained that the wood he had chosen came from Grace's Scottish home. He had managed to track down a family member who still owned a portion of the property and had agreed to sell him just enough of the Scotch pine he needed. The plaque above the entrance read

Crҽidҽamh and Ɖrҽam

the Scottish words for Faith and Family.

The interior held a circle of box benches, Jake led

her to the one at the center back. Burned into the wood were the words from her mother's favorite poem; I will arise and go now, and go to Innisfree...

"Thank you... it's more beautiful than I could have imagined."

Jake lifted the lid to one of the benches, "Even more..."

He laid four wooden slats on the bench... burned into each a name; Jake, Karilyne, Joshua and Jillianne. He lifted the two slats bearing Jake and Karilyne, stood on the bench and snapped them into grooves that had been carved just below the roof's curve. Karilyne handed him the remaining two and he placed them on either side of their names.

"There... now it's complete."

Karilyne smiled and pointed to several other open grooves, "Who are those for?"

Jake stood next to her, his hands in his pockets and shrugged, "For more."

"More… more what?"

"More family, Karilyne."

Karilyne nodded. "Yes… more family."

Jake lifted another lid and retrieved a blanket, two flutes and a bottle of champagne. "Come… sit with me."

Karilyne snuggled under the blanket and Jake poured the champagne. "I thought we should celebrate."

"Oh! That's right… I forgot… it's the Fourth of July!"

"Yes it is, but that's not what I meant." Jake lifted Karilyne's chin. "We are celebrating Jake and Karilyne… all that we have been and all that we will be."

And just beyond the tops of the tall pines that line the yard… past the fields and the fences… down suicide hill and past the wrought iron that surrounds St. James… above Patricia and Kurt's crumb littered quilt… above Jaclyn and Frankie's tangled limbs... above the hummingbird bench, the ducks and the lake, the first rocket of the night lit the sky with a white-hot umbrella of joy.

Fall

Chapter thirty

Patricia hesitated at the bottom of the stairs... she'd only walked down the halls of the second floor twice since she had made the small farm her home. The first time had been a few days after moving in, but after the echoes of her footsteps through each empty room reminded her of just how really alone she was... how alone she would always be... she decided to close the door at the bottom of the stairs and leave the mice and the drafts to wander freely. The second time had been to help a confused owl back through an open window. Today, she was on a mission. She stood in the center of the first room, closed her eyes and pictured pinks and lavenders, a canopy bed and a violin in the corner. In the next room, blues and yellows, a hand-painted headboard and bookshelves. In the bathroom, a claw foot tub and a double vanity for equal mirror time. Two more rooms... one for an office and the other for painting, drawing… creating.

She walked back down the stairs and stopped in front of the fireplace. She held her hands in front of the dying log and pulled her sweater tightly around her. She gently traced the curve of the large urn and smiled. "Things are about to get very noisy around here and I hope that's okay with you. I thought, once, that I would spend my life here alone… just trying to remember the sound of your voice… the feel of your touch but I need to be needed. I need to hear the sound of little girl giggles again. I need to feel the warmth of a man next to me at night. I need to laugh… I need to sing… and, yes, I need to dance."

She carried her suitcase to the front porch and closed the door behind her. A gentle breeze rustled the fall leaves. She sat in the rocking chair, clasped her hands and bowed her head. *God, only you know why you took Peter and Anna from me. I thought I chose this place so I could live the rest of my life alone but I know now that it was you who chose this place and that your plan was never for me to be alone. Thank you for the gifts of Kurt and Shannon and Brigitte ... help me be the wife and mother they deserve.* She raised her head and watched a flock of geese fly through a brilliant blue sky. *And thank you for this perfect day!*

She checked her watch... *I have a ceremony to get to!*

Jaclyn stood in front of the full length mirror that had stood in her mother's bedroom. She had rescued it from the attic corner shortly after Karilyne... and Frankie... had rescued her from her own little corner. She held the new dress in front of her with one hand and swept her hair up with the other. She swayed back and forth and blushed as she remembered her first dance with Frankie. Her only hope when she had moved back to the village had been the gift of a little time with her father. She never imagined that she would find Karilyne, Patricia and her dream job and, in even her wildest dreams, she would never have believed that she would find a good man, a kind man, a gentle, exciting, beautiful man and fall in love in the same little village where she had first known love.

The truck's horn sounded from the drive. Jaclyn leaned out of the upstairs window and waved, "Coming!" She placed her dress back in the dress bag, grabbed the tote that held her shoes, sweater and make-up bag and ran down the stairs.

Karilyne walked barefoot to the gazebo, the steam from her mug swirling into the cool, autumn air. She sat on the stairs, took a sip and looked over the carefully arranged lawn.

The decorations had been kept simple. Patricia had seen Karilyne's wedding photos and asked if it would be ok if they were to create something similar. Not only had it been ok, Karilyne had been thrilled to recreate the day that had meant so much to her and Jake. She had filled baskets with cones from the towering pines, leaves from the maples and golden and burgundy mums.

A tent had been erected with a makeshift dance floor on the opposite side of the property, close enough to Jake's workshop so that the lanterns and the small band Karilyne had hired could use the electricity.

The chairs had been draped in cream colored satin and gathered with burgundy bows that Jaclyn had sewn. Karilyne left the rest of it up to Mother Nature... and she had not disappointed. A beautiful, blue sky and a light breeze that occasionally fanned the flames in the log filled fire pits.

The back door opened and Jake called from the deck, "Hey! Plenty of time for lounging later... Jaclyn just called... the cake is on its way."

"Woo-hoo!! Tell Frankie to pull the truck around to the side so they can unload it directly onto the table."

The cake had been top secret. Jaclyn had given no

indication as to its size, shape or color, but, now, finally Karilyne was finally going to get to see it.

"Come on Jaclyn... just a peak!"

"NO, Karilyne... no one is going to see it till after the ceremony!"

"It's really not fair you know. I showed you all of the decorations."

Jaclyn giggled," You had to... I needed to know what colors to make the ribbons and because you wanted the cake to match."

"And does it?"

"You'll see!"

Karilyne smiled and put her arm around Jaclyn's shoulders. The two women stood looking at the ribbon adorned gazebo.

"It has been one heck of a year!"

"You can say that again..."

"But now, it feels as if everything is just as it should be."

The women sighed in unison.

"So, did she show you the cake?" Patricia joined the pair, her arm encircling Jaclyn's waist.

"No! This is by far the biggest secret ever kept in Allert village."

Patricia laughed, "I know... I don't know what I am looking forward to most... marrying Kurt or seeing the wedding cake!"

Jaclyn rolled her eyes, "The cake... trust me... it's the cake."

"I've seen the cake... I think she's right!" Jillianne wrapped her arms around the group.

"Jilly... you're here!"

"Of course, there is no way I would miss this... besides, Paris is great, but" she pressed her cheek against Karilyne's "there is something about this little village that keeps me coming back."

Karilyne smiled, "Jillianne is studying at the Le Cordon Bleu in Chicago this year and returning to Paris next year."

Jillianne nodded, "Just a short three hour drive from here."

Karilyne was bursting, "We are going to have more than one girls trip for shopping and theater… all four of us!"

"Look out Wacker and Michigan!"

Karilyne checked her watch, "Before we go shopping maybe we should have a wedding… I think we are all set except for, you know, the groom?"

Patricia laughed, "They are on their…."

"Hey… mom!" Brigitte and Shannon ran to Patricia. She had worried that it would be difficult for them to call her mom, that they would worry about 'replacing' their mother, but when she had begun the conversation, it was Kurt's amazing daughters who had taken her by the hands and told her they would never forget their mother any more than she would ever forget Anna. They told her that their mother was an amazing and special person and she would want them to have someone as special as Patricia to be there for them.

Kurt joined the group and kissed Patricia, "Hey beautiful... you ready?"

"I can't wait."

Karilyne spoke over Patricia's shoulder, "Well, you're going to have to... at least an hour. I didn't do all of this so you could get married in your jeans." She motioned to Jake's workshop, "Men in there," then to the house, "women in there." She took Patricia's hand. "Let's have a wedding."

Chapter thirty one

Kurt turned as the guitarist began Pachelbel's canon. Brigitte and Shannon began a slow, measured walk down the satin runner with Patricia a few steps behind. The three were dressed in ankle length, crème colored satin dresses with velvet burgundy ribbons encircling the tops of the empire waists. They carried bouquets of crème colored roses and amethyst colored lilies, complements of the Amante farm. They climbed the few steps of the gazebo and stood in front of Father O'Brien, the girls on either side of Kurt and Patricia.

The small group was seated and Michael began the ceremony.

"Dearly beloved, we are gathered here today to witness the joining of this man and this woman in holy matrimony", Michael stopped and smiled.

"Kurt and Patricia, I have learned that happiness and joy, loss and longing are all drunk from the same cup and we can never be certain which drink we will take next, as everyone gathered here knows all too well. Some sips will be bitter and some sweet. Today we sip the sweet nectar of healing, hope and love. So my prayer for you as you begin this journey is that each day that you are blessed with a sweet sip, you give thanks... thanks for one another, thanks for these beautiful girls and thanks for the friends who have gathered here to celebrate your new beginning. On those days when it seems your cup has nothing to offer but bitter sips... remember the faith, friends and love that brought you to this day." The four standing before him joined hands as he continued with the vows, the pronouncement and the kiss. The small audience erupted with applause and cheers.

Jillianne poured champagne as everyone lined up at the buffet.

Dinner had been a debate... Karilyne wanted Cornish hens, rice pilaf, asparagus or salmon en croute but Patricia said absolutely not... no one was going to be stuck cooking on their day, 'This day belongs to all of us... the wedding is just a small part of the celebration'. So the night before the day, as the men grilled steaks and chicken for dinner, the women peeled, chopped, diced, and created... what else... soups. French onion with gruyere and baguettes. Pasta e Fagiolo with parmesan and garlic toast. Southwest chicken and butternut squash with cheddar and chipotle corn bread. Jaclyn's eclectic mix of vintage soup crocks was stacked at the start of the line and the larger crocks containing the soup were placed evenly down the long table. When the younger Amantes turned up their noses at the soups, Jake produced a package of hot dogs and a bag of potato chips. Karilyne was surprised, "We have hot dogs and chips?"

Jake winked, "I thought we might need them!"

As dinner was winding down and the band was setting up, Frankie and Jaclyn snuck away to the back of the refrigerated truck, lifted the large box that held the cake and placed it onto the table. Jaclyn gave Karilyne a thumbs up. Karilyne lifted her champagne glass, "And now... not to take away from a beautiful ceremony or a delicious dinner, if we do say so ourselves, I think we can agree that the real reason we are all here today is for... The Cake!!!"

The adults cheered and the kids squealed as everyone took their place in front of the table. "Patricia and Kurt," Jaclyn began, "I can't begin to find the words to tell you what your family means to me... to all of us. I hope this cake lets you know." She took a deep breath and, with shaking hands, lifted the box.

The group stood silent for several moments. Jaclyn stood nervously waiting until Patricia broke the silence, whispering through tears of joy "Jaclyn... it's the most beautiful thing I've ever seen... it's perfect!"

And it was. Three tiers covered with antique ivory buttercream told their story in perfect marzipan. It began on either side of the bottom of the first tier; Patricia's station wagon began the trip up the cake while on the opposite side, Kurt's van did as well. Replicas of Patchwork Farm, Kurt's home, Karilyne's Korner, Willow Creek. An apron and white coat. Asparagus stalks, sage leaves, strawberries and busy bees grew and flew on the first and second tier. Hearts, a lake, a flag and fireworks adorned the top tier and, finally, a sandy haired man, a dark haired woman and two small red heads stood inside of a spun sugar gazebo on top.

Karilyne and Patricia wrapped their arms around Jaclyn, "We are blessed to have you in our lives." Kurt wiped a tear from his cheek, cleared his throat and looked at the eager faces of Shannon, Brigitte, Joey, Vinny and Mary Catherine, "So… do we get to cut it?"

Jaclyn laughed, "Absolutely!"

"Yea!!!"

The bottom tier was Karilyne's chocolate-lavender, the middle was Jaclyn's strawberries and cream and the top was Patricia's famous spice and everyone wanted a piece of each.

The band's leader indicated that they were ready whenever Karilyne was. "If I can get all of you to the gazebo one more time before the band begins, Jake and I have gifts for everyone."

Jillianne cleared the cake plates while the group gathered once again.

"I have learned so much from each of you this year. Generosity, patience, understanding.... Mostly I have learned that family transcends the bonds of blood." She turned to point to the words at the gazebo's entrance, "Creideamh... Faith. Dream... family. But Gaelic words often times have many translations. That word also means clan or tribe and through all of the burnt breads, soured soups, concave cakes, laughter and tears, we have indeed become a beautiful, crazy tribe… a family." Jake stood at Karilyne's side holding three packages. He handed one to Patricia, one to Jaclyn and one to Rose. "Please… open them."

Joseph, Vincent, Mary Catherine and the newest member of the Amante family, Theresa Marie had been neatly carved into the wood just under the names Joseph and Rose. Brigitte and Shannon under the names Kurt and Patricia and finally, Francis and Jaclyn with obvious blank spaces beneath. They climbed the steps to the gazebo and Jake snapped each piece into an empty groove. Karilyne smiled, "Perfect."

As the sun began to sink just beyond the wooded edge, Jillianne flipped a switch and the tent's lanterns began to glow as the band began to play. Karilyne stood at the edge of the party watching the guests as they slow danced under the tent, the wind gently lifting the billowing silk in rhythm with the music. Jake slid his arms around her waist and kissed her neck. "What are you thinking about over here... so deep in thought?"

Karilyne rested her head on his shoulder. "Silly... really. I was just thinking that a year ago I thought everything was ending. Being a daughter, being a mother.... being a wife. I thought life had come to an abrupt standstill."

"And now?"

Karilyne turned to look into Jake's eyes, "It's only just begun."

The end

Thank you so much for reading Karilyne's Korner. I hope you enjoyed reading it as much as I enjoyed writing it. Allert Village is based, in part, upon the small village in which I have lived for the last 25 years. The cover which was so beautifully painted by Charlotte Lipp is a replication of two of the original buildings from the 1800's which still stand on the village boulevard. To see actual pictures of the buildings, the Village lake, the bench and St. James, visit my website www.kristywoods.com. You will also find an excerpt from Patricia's Promise, the second in the Allert Village trilogy which will be available this summer!

Please feel free to contact me... I would love to hear from you!

Thanks,

Kristy

53428063R00189

Made in the USA
Lexington, KY
04 July 2016